KaRLSSON
on the Roof

BY **ASTRID LINDGREN**

ILLUSTRATED BY **MINI GREY**

TRANSLATED BY SARAH DEATH

OXFORD
UNIVERSITY PRESS

THE WORLD OF
ASTRID LINDGREN

BOOKS BY ASTRID LINDGREN
ILLUSTRATED BY MINI GREY

Pippi Longstocking

Pippi Longstocking Goes Aboard

Pippi Longstocking in the South Seas

Emil and the Great Escape

Emil and the Sneaky Rat

Emil's Clever Pig

Lotta Says 'No!'

Lotta Makes a Mess

Karlsson Flies Again

Karlsson on the Roof

The World's Best Karlsson

The Children of Noisy Village

Nothing But Fun in Noisy Village

Happy Times in Noisy Village

THE WORLD OF
ASTRID LINDGREN

KaRLSSON
on the Roof

OXFORD
UNIVERSITY PRESS

Great Clarendon Street, Oxford OX2 6DP
Oxford University Press is a department of the University of Oxford.
It furthers the University's objective of excellence in research, scholarship,
and education by publishing worldwide. Oxford is a registered trade mark of
Oxford University Press in the UK and in certain other countries

Translated from the Swedish by Sarah Death
English translation © Sarah Death 2008

First published in 1955 as *Lillebror och Karlsson på taket* by Rabén & Sjögren, Sweden
All foreign rights are handled by The Astrid Lindgren Company, Stockholm, Sweden.
For more information, please contact info@astridlindgren.se

First published in Great Britain by Oxford University Press 1958
First published in this edition 2021 by Oxford University Press

Database right Oxford University Press (maker)

British Library Cataloguing in Publication Data

Data available

ISBN: 978-0-19-277627-3

1 3 5 7 9 10 8 6 4 2

Printed in India

CONTENTS

Karlsson on the Roof

In a perfectly ordinary street in a perfectly ordinary house in Stockholm lives a perfectly ordinary family called Stevenson. It consists of a perfectly ordinary father and a perfectly ordinary mother and three perfectly ordinary children, Seb, Sally, and Smidge.

'I'm not an ordinary Smidge at all,' says Smidge. But he's lying. He most certainly is ordinary. There are so many boys of seven with blue eyes and snub noses and unwashed ears and trousers that always have holes in the knees, so Smidge most definitely is perfectly ordinary, there's no question about it.

1

Seb is fifteen and likes football and isn't getting on very well at school, so he's perfectly ordinary, too; and Sally is fourteen and has her hair in a ponytail like other perfectly ordinary girls.

There's only one person in the whole house who isn't ordinary, and that's Karlsson on the Roof. He lives up on the roof, Karlsson, and that's not very ordinary, for a start. It may be different in other parts of the world, but in Stockholm you scarcely ever find anyone living in a special little house up on the roof. Yet that's precisely what Karlsson does. He is a very small, round, determined gentleman, and he can fly. Everybody can fly in aeroplanes and helicopters, but Karlsson is the only one who can fly all by himself. Karlsson simply turns a winder somewhere in front of his tummy button, and hey presto! A clever little motor on his back starts whirring. Karlsson stands there for a moment while his motor revs up. And then—when his propellor is whizzing round fast enough—Karlsson takes off and hovers away, as fine and stately as a high court judge, if you can imagine a high court judge with a propellor on his back.

Karlsson is very happy in his little house up on the roof. In the evenings he sits on his front step and smokes his pipe and looks at the stars. Of course, you can see the stars much better from up on the roof than anywhere else in the building, so it's strange, really, that not more people live on roofs. But the people who rent the flats in the house don't know you can live on roofs; they don't even know that Karlsson has his little house up there, because it's so well hidden behind the big chimney. And anyway, most people don't notice houses as small as Karlsson's, even if they trip over them. A chimney sweep once caught sight of Karlsson's house as he was about to sweep the chimney, and he was quite astonished.

'That's strange,' he said to himself, 'there's a house up here. Who would have thought it, there's a house up on the roof, but however did it get here?'

Then he set about sweeping the chimney and totally forgot the house, and never thought of it again.

It was certainly a stroke of luck for Smidge, getting to know Karlsson, because whenever Karlsson flew in, things turned exciting and there were adventures to be had. Perhaps Karlsson thought it was a stroke of luck getting to know Smidge, too, because after all, it can't always be much fun living all alone in a house without anyone else realizing you're there. It must be nice to have someone to call out 'Heysan hopsan, Karlsson,' whenever you fly in.

This is how Karlsson and Smidge met.

It was one of those difficult days when it wasn't the least fun being Smidge. Normally it was rather nice being Smidge, because he was the pet and darling of the whole family, and they all spoilt him as much as they could. But there were days when everything went wrong. On days like that you were told off by Mum for making more holes in your trousers, and Sally said, 'Blow your nose, kid,' and Dad was cross because you were late home from school.

'Why must you hang about the streets?' Dad asked. Hang about the streets? What Dad didn't know was that Smidge had met a dog. A lovely, friendly dog that had sniffed at Smidge and wagged his tail and looked as if he would like to be Smidge's dog.

If it had been up to Smidge he could have

been Smidge's dog, straight away. But the problem was that Mum and Dad didn't want a dog in the house. And anyway, a lady turned up just then and called, 'Here, Ricky,' and Smidge realized this couldn't be his dog, after all.

'Doesn't seem to be any chance of me getting a dog as long as I live,' Smidge said bitterly, that day everything was going wrong. 'Mum, you've got Dad, and Seb and Sally always stick together, but I haven't got anybody.'

'But, Smidge, love, you've got all of us,' said Mum.

'Oh no, I haven't,' said Smidge even more bitterly, because he suddenly felt as if he had nobody in the whole wide world.

There was one thing he did have, though. He had his own room, so that was where he went.

It was a beautiful, light spring evening, and the window was open. The white curtains were swaying gently to and fro, just as if they were waving to the small, pale stars up there in the spring sky. Smidge went over to the window and looked out. He thought about that friendly dog and wondered what he was doing now: whether he was lying in a dog basket in a kitchen somewhere, and whether a boy—some other boy, not Smidge—was sitting on the floor beside him, patting his shaggy head and saying, 'Good dog, Ricky.'

Smidge gave a big sigh. Then he heard a faint buzzing sound. The buzzing grew louder, and all at once, a fat little man flew slowly past the window. It was Karlsson on the Roof, but Smidge didn't know that, of course.

Karlsson merely gave Smidge a long look and went sailing by. He took a little detour over the roof of the house opposite, did a circuit of the chimney and then headed back to Smidge's window. He had got up speed now, and went whistling past Smidge almost like a little jet plane. He went whizzing past several times, while Smidge just stood there waiting, feeling his tummy flutter with excitement, because it wasn't every day of the week he had fat little men flying past his window. Finally Karlsson came to a halt, right outside the window ledge.

'Heysan hopsan,' he said. 'Mind if I drop in for a while?'

'Oh no, please do,' said Smidge. 'It must be hard to fly like that,' he went on.

'Not for me,' said Karlsson importantly. 'For me, it's not hard at all. Because I'm the world's best stunt flyer. But I wouldn't recommend any old sack of hay to try it.'

Smidge had a definite feeling he was 'any old sack of hay', and decided on the spot not to try copying Karlsson's flying stunts.

'What's your name?' asked Karlsson.

'Smidge,' said Smidge. 'Though my real name is Steven Stevenson.'

'Imagine names being so different—mine's Karlsson,' said Karlsson. 'Plain Karlsson and nothing else. Well, heysan hopsan, Smidge.'

'Heysan hopsan, Karlsson,' said Smidge.

'How old are you?' asked Karlsson.

'Seven,' said Smidge.

'Good. You carry on with that,' said Karlsson.

He briskly swung one of his fat little legs over Smidge's window ledge and stepped into the room.

'How old are you, then?' asked Smidge, thinking Karlsson seemed rather childish for a grown-up man.

'Me?' said Karlsson. 'I'm a man in my prime, that's all I can say.'

Smidge didn't really know what that meant—being a man in his prime. He wondered whether he might be a man in his prime as well, without knowing it, and asked cautiously:

'Which bit is the prime?'

'All of it,' said Karlsson with satisfaction. 'For me, at any rate. I'm a handsome, thoroughly clever, perfectly plump man in my prime,' he went on.

Then he took Smidge's steam engine from its place on the bookshelf.

'Shall we get this going?' he suggested.

'I'm not supposed to,' said Smidge. 'Dad says either he or Seb must be here when I have it running.'

'Dad or Seb or Karlsson on the Roof,' said Karlsson. 'He's the world's best steam engine driver, Karlsson is. You tell your dad.'

He grabbed up the bottle of methylated spirits from beside the steam engine, filled the little spirit lamp and lit it. Although he was the world's best steam engine driver, he clumsily spilled a whole little lake of methylated spirits on the bookcase, and merry blue flames danced around the engine as the lake caught fire. Smidge gave a shriek and dashed across the room.

'Easy now, take it easy,' said Karlsson, holding up a plump hand to keep Smidge at bay.

But Smidge couldn't take it easy as long as he could see things burning. He grabbed an old rag and smothered the merry little flames. Where they had been dancing, there were now two big scorch marks on the varnish of the bookcase.

'Oh dear, look at the bookcase,' said Smidge anxiously. 'What's Mum going to say?'

'Ah, that's a mere trifle,' said Karlsson on the Roof. 'A few insignificant marks on a bookcase—a mere trifle, you tell your mum.'

He was kneeling beside the steam engine, and his eyes were shining.

'We'll soon get some proper chuff from it,' he said.

And he was right. The steam machine was soon working away. Chuff-chuff-chuff, it went. Oh, it was the splendidest steam engine you could imagine, and Karlsson looked so proud and happy, as if he'd built it himself.

'I've got to check the safety valve,' said Karlsson, fiddling eagerly with a little widget. 'There are always accidents if you don't check the safety valve.'

Chuff-chuff-chuff, went the steam engine. It puffed faster and faster and faster, chuffa-chuffa-chuffa. In the end it sounded as if it was galloping, and Karlsson's eyes sparkled. Smidge stopped worrying about the marks on the bookcase; he felt terribly happy about his steam engine and about Karlsson, who was the world's best steam-engine driver and had checked the safety valve so well.

'Oh yes, Smidge,' said Karlsson, 'we've got a real chuff-chuff-chuffer here! The world's best steam engine drive—'

He didn't get any further, because at that moment there came a huge bang, and suddenly

there was no steam engine any longer, just bits of steam engine scattered all over the room.

'It exploded,' declared Karlsson with delight, as if that was the greatest trick you could ever expect a steam engine to perform. 'Well I never, it exploded! What a bang, eh?'

But Smidge couldn't feel glad. His eyes filled with tears.

'My steam engine,' he said. 'It's broken.'

'That's a mere trifle,' said Karlsson, with a careless wave of his chubby little hand. 'You can soon get a new one.'

'Where can I?' asked Smidge.

'I've got thousands up at my place.'

'What do you mean, up at your place?' said Smidge.

'Up at my house, on the roof,' said Karlsson.

'You've got a house on the roof?' asked Smidge. 'With thousands of steam engines in it?'

'Yes, there must be at least a few hundred,' answered Karlsson.

'Ooh, I'd love to see your house,' said Smidge. It sounded such a wonderful idea: a little house up on the roof, with Karlsson living in it.

'Just think, a house full of steam engines,'

said Smidge. 'Thousands of them.'

'Yes, I haven't counted exactly how many I've got left, but there are definitely several dozen,' said Karlsson. 'They explode from time to time, you know, but I definitely always have a couple of dozen left.'

'Well maybe I could have one, then,' said Smidge.

'Of course,' said Karlsson. 'Of course!'

'Right now?' Smidge asked.

'Well, I'd need to look it over a bit first,' said Karlsson. 'Check the safety valve and that sort of thing. Easy now, take it easy! You'll get it another day.'

Smidge began collecting up the pieces of what had once been his steam engine.

'I wonder what Dad will say,' he muttered anxiously.

Karlsson raised his eyebrows in surprise.

'About the steam engine,' he said. 'A mere trifle that he doesn't need to worry about in the least, tell him that from me. I'd tell him myself, if I had time to stay and meet him. But now I've got to get home and see to my house.'

'It was fun having you here,' said Smidge.

'Apart from the steam engine . . . Will you be coming back another day?'

'Easy now, take it easy,' said Karlsson, turning the winder that was just in front of his tummy button. His motor started coughing and Karlsson stood there waiting for enough lift to steer properly.

'My motor's coughing,' he said. 'I need to get to the garage for a good greasing. Could do it myself, of course,' he added, 'since I'm the world's best motor mechanic, but I haven't got time . . . no, I think I'll book myself into the garage.'

Smidge thought that would be the most sensible thing to do, too.

Karlsson headed off through the open window, his tubby little body clearly outlined against the star-dotted spring sky.

'Heysan hopsan, Smidge,' he said, waving his chubby hand.

And with that, Karlsson was gone.

Karlsson Builds
a Tower

'**I** told you, he's called Karlsson and he lives up on the roof,' said Smidge. 'What's funny about that? People can live where they like, can't they?'

'Now don't be silly, Smidge,' said Mum. 'You nearly scared the life out of us. Don't you see, you could have been killed when your steam engine exploded?'

'Yes, but anyway, Karlsson is the world's best steam engine driver,' said Smidge, giving his mother a serious look. He had to make her understand that you couldn't say no, not when the world's best steam engine driver offered to set your steam engine going.

'You have to take responsibility for what you did, Smidge,' said Dad, 'not blame it on someone called Karlsson on the Roof, who doesn't exist.'

'Oh yes he does,' said Smidge.

'And he can fly,' said Seb with a laugh.

'Yes, imagine that,' said Smidge. 'I hope he comes back, so you can see for yourself.'

'Let's hope he comes tomorrow,' said Sally. 'I'll give you a krona, Smidge, if I get to see Karlsson on the Roof.'

'He definitely won't come tomorrow,' said Smidge, 'because he's got to go into the garage for a good greasing.'

'Never mind greasing, you could do with a good hiding,' said Mum. 'Look at the state of the bookcase!'

'That's a mere trifle, Karlsson says!'

Smidge flicked his fingers in the same superior sort of way as Karlsson had done, to make Mum understand that the bookcase episode really wasn't anything to make a fuss about. But Mum wasn't impressed.

'Oh he does, does he?' she asked. 'Tell Karlsson that if he sticks his nose in here again,

I'll give him a greasing he'll never forget.'

Smidge didn't reply. He thought it was dreadful of Mum to talk like that about the world's best steam engine driver. But it was no more than he expected on a day like today, when they had clearly all decided to make things difficult.

Smidge suddenly found himself longing for Karlsson. Karlsson who was happy and cheerful and flicked his fingers and said accidents were a mere trifle that you didn't need to worry about. Smidge really did long for Karlsson. But he also felt a bit uneasy. What if Karlsson never came back?

'Easy now, take it easy,' Smidge told himself, just like Karlsson had done. Karlsson had promised.

And Karlsson was someone you could rely on, that was obvious. Just a few days later, he turned up again. Smidge was lying on his front on the floor, reading, when he heard that whirr again, and Karlsson came buzzing through the open window like a giant bumblebee. He hummed a happy little song as he whirred round the walls. Now and then he stopped to look at the pictures. He put his head on one side and squinted.

'Pretty pictures,' he said. 'Extremely pretty pictures! But maybe not quite as pretty as mine.'

Smidge had leapt up from the floor, hardly able to contain his excitement. He was so glad Karlsson had come back.

'Have you got a lot of pictures up at your house?' he asked.

'Thousands,' said Karlsson. 'Paint them myself, in my spare time. All over cockerels and birds and other pretty stuff. I'm the world's best cockerel painter,' said Karlsson, coming in to land beside Smidge with an elegant turn.

'Er . . . Karlsson,' said Smidge, 'how about . . . can I come up with you and see your house and steam engines and pictures?'

'Of course,' said Karlsson. 'Definitely! You'd be most welcome. Another day.'

'Soon?' begged Smidge.

'Easy now, take it easy,' said Karlsson. 'I need to do a bit of cleaning up first, but it won't take long. The world's best speedy cleaner, can you guess who that is?' asked Karlsson mischievously.

'Could it be you?' said Smidge.

'Could be,' shouted Karlsson, 'could be . . . don't doubt it for a moment. The world's best speedy cleaner is Karlsson on the Roof, simply everybody knows that.'

And Smidge could well believe Karlsson was 'the world's best' at everything. He was the world's best playmate, too, for sure; you just knew he was. Kris and Jemima were all right, but they weren't as exciting as Karlsson on the Roof. Smidge decided to tell Kris and Jemima about Karlsson the next time they walked home from school together. Kris always talked a lot about his dog, whose name was Woof. Smidge had been jealous of Kris for ages, because of that dog.

But if he starts going on about Woof tomorrow, like he always does, I shall tell him about Karlsson, thought Smidge. 'What's Woof compared to Karlsson on the Roof?' I shall say.

But there was still nothing Smidge longed for more than a dog of his own.

Karlsson interrupted his thoughts.

'I feel in the mood for a bit of fun,' he said, looking around with curiosity. 'Haven't you got another steam engine?'

Smidge shook his head. The steam engine, that reminded him! Now he had Karlsson here, Mum and Dad could see that he existed. Seb and Sally, too, if they were at home.

'Do you want to come and say hello to my mum and dad?' asked Smidge.

'Delighted,' said Karlsson. 'It'll be nice for them to meet me, handsome and altogether clever as I am!'

Karlsson strutted back and forward across the floor, looking pleased with himself.

'Perfectly plump, too,' he added. 'A man in his prime. Be nice for your mum to meet me.'

Just then, Smidge caught the first waft of frying meatballs from the kitchen, and he knew it would soon be time for dinner. Smidge decided to wait until after dinner to let Karlsson meet his mum and dad. It's never a good idea to disturb mothers when they are frying meatballs. What's more, Mum and Dad might decide to say something to Karlsson about the steam engine and the scorch marks on the bookcase. And that had to be prevented at all costs. At the dinner table, Smidge would somehow cunningly get his parents to understand how you behave towards the world's best steam engine driver. He just needed a bit of time. After dinner—that would be fine. He'd take the whole family into his room.

'Right, see for yourselves, here's Karlsson on the Roof,' he would say. They would be astonished, and what fun it would be to see just how astonished they were.

Karlsson had finished strutting. He was standing there, sniffing the air like a retriever.

'Meatballs,' he said, 'I *do* like dear little, yummy little meatballs.'

Smidge felt a bit awkward. There was really only one answer you could give to a comment like that. 'Do you want to stay for dinner?' was what he ought to say. But he daren't just turn up with Karlsson at the dinner table, unannounced. It was quite a different matter when Kris or Jemima came round. Then it was all right to come along at the last minute, even if the rest of the family were already sitting round the table, and say, 'Please, Mum, Kris and Jemima can stay for some pancakes, too, can't they?'

But a completely unknown, fat little man,

who had wrecked a steam engine and scorched the bookcase—no, that just wouldn't do.

And now that fat little man had just declared that he loved yummy little meatballs. It was up to Smidge to make sure he got some, otherwise he might not want to be with Smidge any more. Oh dear, an awful lot depended on Mum's meatballs!

'Wait here a minute,' said Smidge, 'and I'll pop out to the kitchen and get you some.'

Karlsson nodded in contentment.

'Good,' he said. 'Good! But hurry up. You don't get full up just looking at pictures—without cockerels or anything!'

Smidge slipped out into the kitchen. Mum was standing at the stove, wearing a checked apron and enveloped in the most wonderful smell of meatballs. She was shaking the big frying pan over the gas flame, and the pan was as full as can be of lovely little brown meatballs, all jumping about.

'Hello, Smidge,' said Mum. 'We'll be eating soon.'

'Please, Mum, can I have a few meatballs on a saucer, to take into my room?' said Smidge in his persuading voice.

'But, darling, we'll be eating in a couple of minutes,' Mum said.

'Oh, please let me,' said Smidge. 'I'll explain why after dinner.'

'All right then,' said Mum. 'Just a few!'

She put six meatballs on a little plate. Oh, they smelt so wonderful, and they were small and brown and lovely, just as they should be. Smidge carried the plate carefully in both hands and hurried back to his room.

'Here, Karlsson,' he said as he opened the door.

But Karlsson had vanished. There stood Smidge with the meatballs, but no Karlsson was to be seen. Smidge was dreadfully disappointed; everything suddenly seemed to go flat.

'He's gone,' he said out loud to himself.

But then . . .

'Squeak,' he suddenly heard someone say. 'Squeak!'

Smidge looked round. Right down at the foot of his bed—under the covers—he saw a fat little lump, and it was moving. That was where the squeaks were coming from. And a second later, Karlsson poked a red face out from between the sheets.

'Hee hee,' said Karlsson. '"He's gone," you said. "He's gone"—hee hee, I haven't gone at all, you know. I was only pretending.'

Then he spotted the meatballs. Like a shot he turned the winder on his tummy, his motor started to whirr, and Karlsson came flying through the air, heading straight for the plate. He snatched a meatball as he passed, rose quickly up to the ceiling and circled the light, happily munching the meatball.

'Delicious,' he said. 'Mighty tasty meatball! You might almost think the world's best meatball maker had made it, though we *know* he can't have done,' said Karlsson. And then he made a lightning dive back down to the plate and snatched another one.

Just then, Mum called from the kitchen:

'Smidge, dinner's ready, hurry up and wash your hands and come!'

'I've got to go again,' said Smidge, putting down the plate. 'But I'll be back soon. Promise you'll wait for me!'

'Yes, but what'll I do in the meantime?' asked Karlsson, landing beside Smidge with a reproachful little thud. 'I need some fun while I'm waiting. Are you sure you haven't got any more steam engines?'

'No,' said Smidge, 'but you can borrow my building set.'

'Just the thing,' said Karlsson.

Smidge got his building set out of the toy cupboard. It was a really nice set with lots of different parts you could fix together to make different things.

'Here you are,' he said. 'You can build cars and cranes and all sorts of things . . . '

'Think I don't know what you can do and what you can't?' asked Karlsson. 'I *am* the world's best putter-together of building sets, you know.' Then he quickly crammed another meatball into his mouth and pounced on the building set.

'Let's see, let's see,' he said, emptying all the bits and pieces onto the floor.

Smidge had to go, although he would far rather have stayed and watched the world's best putter-together of building sets get down to work.

The last thing he saw, as he turned round in the doorway, was Karlsson sitting on the floor, singing happily to himself:

'Hurrah, how good at building I am . . . hurrah, how ever so clever I am . . . And more or less perfectly plump . . . yum!'

He sang the last part just as soon as he had swallowed the fourth meatball.

Mum and Dad and Seb and Sally were already sitting at the table. Smidge slipped into his place and picked up his napkin.

'Promise me something, Mum, and you too, Dad,' he said.

'What is it you want us to promise?' asked Mum.

'Promise first,' said Smidge.

Dad didn't really want to agree to promise, just like that.

'Who knows, you might be wanting me to promise you a dog again,' he said.

'No, it isn't a dog,' said Smidge, 'though it would be great if you did promise that. No, it's something else, and nothing bad at all. Promise you'll promise!'

'Oh all right, we promise,' Mum said.

'OK, now you've promised not to say anything to Karlsson on the Roof about the steam engine,' said Smidge, relieved.

'Ha,' replied Sally, 'how can they say anything at all to Karlsson, since they never get to see him?'

'But they *will* get to see him,' said Smidge triumphantly. 'After dinner. He's in my room right now.'

'Think I just choked on a meatball,' said Seb. 'Are you telling us he's in your room right now? Karlsson?'

'Yes, he is, so there!'

It was a moment of triumph for Smidge. Oh, if only they'd hurry up and finish eating, then they'd see . . .

Mum smiled.

'It really will be nice for us all to meet Karlsson,' she said.

'Yes, Karlsson said the same,' Smidge assured her. At last they finished their fruit salad. At last Mum got up from the table. Now the big moment had arrived.

'Come on, all of you,' said Smidge.

'No need to hurry us up,' said Sally. 'I can hardly wait to see this Karlsson.'

Smidge went first.

'Remember what you all promised,' he said before he opened the door to his room. 'Not a word about the steam engine!'

He pushed down the door handle and opened the door.

Karlsson was gone. Utterly gone. There was no fat little lump under the covers on Smidge's bed.

But in the middle of the floor, a tower rose up from the jumble of building bricks. A very tall, thin tower. Though Karlsson could of course build cranes and other things, this time he had contented himself with piling the bricks on top of each other, to make this very tall, very thin tower. The top of the tower was decorated with something that was obviously supposed to look like a dome. It was a little round meatball.

Karlsson Plays Tents

Smidge had a difficult few minutes. Mum didn't like her meatballs being used as ornaments, and she thought it was Smidge who had decorated the tower so nicely like that, of course.

'Karlsson on the Roof . . .' began Smidge, but Dad said sternly:

'We'll have no more Karlsson fantasies, thank you, Smidge.'

Seb and Sally just laughed.

'That Karlsson,' said Seb. 'Trust him to shove off just when we wanted to say hello!'

31

Smidge sadly ate the meatball and tidied his building bricks into their box. There was no point saying any more about Karlsson just now. But things felt empty without him, very empty.

'Let's have coffee and forget about Karlsson,' said Dad, giving Smidge a comforting pat on the cheek. They always had coffee in front of the fire in the sitting room, and they did the same this evening, although it was spring, light and warm, and the lime trees in the street outside were sprouting little green leaves. Smidge didn't like coffee, but he liked sitting with Mum and Dad and Seb and Sally in front of the fire.

'Shut your eyes a minute, Mum,' said Smidge, once Mum had put down the coffee tray on the little table in front of the open fire.

'Why have I got to shut my eyes?'

'So you don't see me eating sugar, of course, and I'm just going to take a lump,' Smidge said.

He had a very definite feeling that he needed something to comfort him. Why had Karlsson gone off like that? You just couldn't do that— vanish and leave nothing behind but a little meatball.

Smidge sat in his favourite seat by the hearth, as near the fire as he could get. This after-dinner coffee time was almost the best bit of the day. You could talk to Mum and Dad, and they listened to what you said, which they didn't always have time to do otherwise. He liked listening to Seb and Sally too: the way they teased each other and talked about their 'studies'. 'Studies' were clearly very different and much posher than the little school Smidge went to.

Smidge wanted to talk about his 'studies' too, but nobody except Mum and Dad were interested in those. Seb and Sally just laughed in their annoying way. But it wasn't worth them trying to annoy him, because he was a genius at annoying them back—you *had* to be, if you had a brother like Seb and a sister like Sally.

'Well, Smidge, how did you get on in class today?' Mum asked.

That wasn't the sort of talk Smidge liked. But since Mum hadn't said anything about the sugar lump just now, he supposed he'd have to put up with her asking.

'Fine, of *course*,' he said grumpily.

He couldn't stop thinking about Karlsson.

How could anyone expect him to remember anything about his school work, when he didn't know what had happened to Karlsson?

'What were you doing?' asked Dad.

Smidge felt annoyed. Were they going to keep on like that? That wasn't why you all sat relaxing round the fire together—to make people talk about their school work.

'The alphabet,' Smidge said hastily. 'The whole alphabet, and I *know* that—A comes first, and then all the other letters!'

He helped himself to another sugar lump and thought about Karlsson again. They could chatter and buzz around him as much as they liked; Smidge kept thinking about Karlsson and wondering if he would ever see him again.

It was Sally who interrupted his reverie.

'Smidge, are you listening? Do you want to earn twenty-five öre pocket money?'

It eventually sank in what she was saying. Smidge had nothing against earning 25 öre, but it depended what Sally wanted him to do for it.

'Twenty-five öre's not enough,' he said cockily. 'Everything's so expensive these days. How much do you think a fifty öre ice cream costs, for example?'

'Er . . . I'm guessing here,' said Sally knowingly, 'but could it be fifty öre?'

'Yes, you're right,' said Smidge. 'So you must see that twenty-five öre isn't enough.'

'But you don't even know how you're going to earn it yet,' said Sally. 'You haven't got to do anything—just *not* do something.'

'What shall I not do?'

'You won't show yourself in the sitting room this evening.'

'Charlie's coming round, you know,' said Seb. 'Sally's new boyfriend!'

Smidge nodded. Aha, so that was the way they'd planned it. Mum and Dad were going to the cinema, and Seb was off to a football match, and Sally could sit cooing in the sitting room and Smidge would be banished to his bedroom—all for the miserly sum of 25 öre. A fine family he had!

'What sort of ears has he got?' Smidge asked. 'Do they stick out as much as your old boyfriend's?'

That was the way to get Sally annoyed.

'Hear that, Mum?' she said. 'Now do you see

why I want Smidge out of the way? He scares away anybody I invite round.'

'Oh, I'm sure he doesn't,' Mum said weakly. She didn't like it when her children squabbled.

'He does, though,' Sally assured her. 'He scared away Pete, didn't he? He stood gawping at him for ages and then he said: "Sally doesn't like ears like that, you know." So it's hardly surprising Pete never came back, is it?'

'Easy now, take it easy,' said Smidge in exactly the same tone of voice as Karlsson. 'Easy now, take it easy! I will stay in my room, and I'll do it for nothing. I don't want to get paid for people not having to see me.'

'Great,' said Sally. 'Let's shake on it! Shake on you not showing yourself all evening!'

'Done!' said Smidge. 'I'm not that keen on all your Charlies. In fact, I'd pay twenty-five öre to get out of seeing them!'

Some time later, Smidge really was in his room—totally free of charge. Mum and Dad had gone to the cinema, Seb had made himself scarce, and if Smidge opened the door, he could hear a faint murmur from the sitting room. It came from Sally, who was in there chatting with Charlie. Smidge opened the door a few times and tried to make out what they were saying, but he couldn't. So he went over to the window and looked out into the twilight. He peered down into the street to see if Kris and Jemima were playing out. But there were only a couple of big boys having a fight. It was pretty interesting, and he enjoyed it as long as the fight lasted, but sadly the boys soon stopped fighting and then everything was boring again.

Then he heard a heavenly sound. He heard the whirr of a motor and a second later Karlsson came sailing in through the window.

'Heysan hopsan, Smidge,' he said casually.

'Heysan hopsan, Karlsson,' said Smidge. 'Where did you get to?'

'Eh? What do you mean?' asked Karlsson.

'Well, you disappeared, didn't you?' said Smidge. 'When you were supposed to be meeting Mum and Dad. Why did you go?'

Karlsson put his hands on his hips and looked very cross.

'Huh, I've never heard anything like it,' he said. 'Aren't I allowed to go and see to my house? A house owner needs to see to his house, doesn't he, otherwise where would we be? Can I help it if your mum and dad want to pay their respects to me just when I'm busy seeing to my house?'

He looked around the room.

'Talking of houses,' he said, 'where's my tower? Who's wrecked my lovely tower and where's my meatball?'

Smidge began to stammer.

'I-I didn't think you were coming back,' he said anxiously.

'No, that's obvious,' said Karlsson. 'The world's best tower builder builds a tower, and what happens? Does somebody put a little fence round the tower and guard it to make sure it stays there for ever? No, not on your life! They pull it down and wreck it, that's what they do, and eat up other people's meatballs!'

Karlsson went over to a stool, sat down, and sulked.

'But surely that's a mere trifle?' said Smidge, flicking his fingers the Karlsson way. 'It's nothing to worry about.'

'Easy for you to say,' said Karlsson indignantly. 'It's so easy to pull everything down, and then just say it's a mere trifle and there's an end to it. But what about me? I built that tower with these poor little hands of mine!'

He thrust his podgy hands under Smidge's nose. Then he sat back down on the stool and sulked worse than ever.

'Count me out,' he said. 'Count me out if it's going to be like this.'

Smidge felt desperate. He stood there not knowing what to do. There was a long silence. In the end, Karlsson said:

'If I got some little present I might cheer up again. Can't be sure, but I *might* cheer up if someone gave me a little present.'

Smidge ran over to the table and started rummaging eagerly in the drawer, because he had some very nice things in there. He had his stamps and his marbles and his coloured crayons and his tin soldiers. And there was a pocket torch he was very fond of.

'Would you like this?' he said, holding out the torch for Karlsson to see.

Karlsson snatched it in a flash.

'This is just the sort of thing it would have to be, to cheer me up,' he said. 'It's not as good as my tower, but if I can have it I shall try to cheer up a *bit*, at any rate.'

'You can have it,' said Smidge.

'I suppose it works?' said Karlsson suspiciously, pressing the switch. And yes, the torch shone, and Karlsson's eyes started shining too.

'Just think, when I'm walking round the roof on autumn evenings and it's all dark, I can shine this and find my way home to my little house and not get lost among the chimney stacks,' he said, patting the torch.

Smidge felt very pleased to hear Karlsson say that. He only wished he could go with Karlsson one day on one of his roof walks and see him shine the torch in the dark.

'Heysan hopsan, Smidge, I've cheered up again now,' said Karlsson. 'Fetch your mum and dad, and they can say hello to me.'

'They've gone to the cinema,' said Smidge.

'Gone to the cinema! When they could be meeting *me*?' said Karlsson in amazement.

'Yes, Sally's the only one at home . . . With her new boyfriend. They're in the sitting room, and I'm not allowed to go in there.'

'What's that?' shouted Karlsson. 'Not allowed

to go where you want? I won't let us put up with that for a single minute. Come on . . .'

'Yes, but I promised,' said Smidge.

'And I promise, that if something's unfair, HawkEye Karlsson will be down on it just like that,' said Karlsson. 'What *exactly* did you promise?'

'I promised not to show myself in the sitting room all evening.'

'And you won't show yourself,' said Karlsson, 'but I expect you'd rather like to see Sally's new boyfriend?' 'Well yes I would, actually,' said Smidge eagerly. 'She had one before whose ears stuck out like jug handles. I want to see what sort of ears this new one's got.'

'Oh yes, so do I,' said Karlsson. 'Just give me a moment, and I'll jiggery-poke out something. The world's best jiggery-poker—that's Karlsson on the Roof.'

He looked round the room.

'That's it,' he said, nodding. 'A blanket . . . That's exactly what we need. I just knew I'd be able to jiggery-poke out something.'

'What is it you've jiggery-poked, then?' asked Smidge.

'You promised not to show yourself in the sitting room all evening, right? But if you're under a blanket, you're not showing yourself.'

'No . . . but . . . ' began Smidge.

'If you're under a blanket, you're not showing yourself. No "buts",' said Karlsson firmly. 'If I'm under a blanket, I'm not showing myself either, and Sally's only got herself to blame. Since she's being so stupid, she won't get to see me, poor, poor little Sally!'

He grabbed up the blanket from Smidge's bed and threw it over his head.

'Come in, come in,' he shouted. 'Come into my tent!'

Smidge crawled under the blanket, while Karlsson stood inside it, giggling smugly.

'I don't expect Sally said anything about not wanting to see a tent in the sitting room? Everybody's always pleased to see a tent, aren't they? Especially one with a light shining inside,' said Karlsson, switching on the torch.

Smidge wasn't so sure Sally would be all that pleased about the tent, but for himself he thought it was mysterious and exciting to be under the blanket with Karlsson and the lighted torch.

Smidge thought they'd be better off staying where they were and playing tents and not bothering about Sally, but Karlsson didn't agree.

'I can't stand unfairness,' he said. 'I'm going into the sitting room, come what may.'

So the tent began walking towards the door. All Smidge had to do was shuffle along with it. A plump little hand stuck out to grasp the door handle and opened the door very quietly and carefully. The tent moved out into the hall, which was only divided from the sitting room by a heavy curtain.

'Easy now, take it easy,' whispered Karlsson. And without making a sound, the tent went gliding across the hall floor and stopped at the curtain. The murmur of voices could be heard a little more clearly now, but still not so clearly that you could make out any words. The sitting room light was turned off; Sally and her Charlie were obviously happy with the dim, dusky light from outside.

'That's good,' whispered Karlsson. 'It means the light of my torch will show up better.'

For now, at any rate, he had the torch switched off.

'Because we're going to be a nice surprise,' whispered Karlsson, beaming under the blanket.

Slowly, slowly, the tent came gliding from behind the curtain. Sally and Charlie were sitting on the little sofa against the opposite wall; slowly, slowly, the tent headed that way.

'I like you, Sally,' Smidge heard a boy's voice say gruffly—how soppy he was, that Charlie!

'Do you?' said Sally, and it all went quiet again.

The dark shape of the tent moved across the floor; slowly and unstoppably it headed for the sofa, getting closer and closer; now it was only a few steps away, but the two of them sitting there saw and heard nothing.

'Do you like me, Sally?' said Sally's Charlie bashfully.

He never got an answer. For just at that moment the light from a torch cut through the grey shadows of the room and hit him full in the face. He leapt up, Sally screamed, and there was much giggling and a thudding of feet running hastily back towards the hall.

You can't see anything when you've just been dazzled by torchlight. But you can *hear*. And Sally and her Charlie heard the laughter, a wild, delighted laughter bubbling up, over by the curtain.

'It's my horrid little brother,' said Sally. 'I'll give him . . . '

Smidge giggled fit to burst.

'Of course she likes you,' he shouted. 'Why shouldn't she? Sally likes *all* boys, so there!'

Then there was a crash, and a bit more giggling. 'Easy now, take it easy,' whispered

Karlsson, as the tent toppled over on its wild flight to the door.

Smidge took it as easy as he could, although the laughter was still bubbling inside him, and Karlsson had fallen right on top of him and he didn't really know which legs were his and which were Karlsson's, and he knew Sally would get them any moment now.

They struggled to their feet as fast as they could and rushed to Smidge's room in total panic, because Sally was right on their tail.

'Easy now, take it easy,' whispered Karlsson, his stumpy little legs pounding like drumsticks under the blanket. 'The world's best sprinter, that's Karlsson on the Roof!' he whispered, but he sounded quite out of breath.

Smidge could run pretty well, too. And there was certainly no time to lose. At the very last second they made it through the door to Smidge's room. Karlsson quickly turned the key and stood there looking pleased, sniggering silently as Sally hammered on the door.

'Just you wait till I get hold of you, Smidge,' shouted Sally angrily.

'But I didn't show myself, all the same,'

shouted Smidge back. And more giggling came from behind the door.

There were *two* people giggling—Sally could have heard that, if she hadn't been so cross.

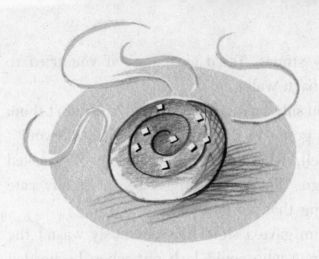

Karlsson Makes a Bet

Smidge came home from school one day looking very indignant, with a big bump on his forehead. Mum was in the kitchen, and she was just as shocked by the bump as Smidge had hoped she would be.

'Smidge, love, whatever's happened?' she said, putting her arms round him.

'Kris threw stones at me,' said Smidge angrily.

'Goodness gracious,' said Mum, 'what a bad boy! Why didn't you come straight in and tell me?'

Smidge shrugged.

'What good would it have done? You can't

throw stones. You'd even miss if you tried to hit a barn wall.'

'You silly sausage!' said Mum. 'You didn't think I was going to throw stones at Kris, did you?'

'Well, what else would you throw?' asked Smidge. 'There's nothing else, or at any rate nothing that works so well.'

Mum gave a sigh. Kris obviously wasn't the only one who could lash out when he needed to. Her own little darling wasn't a bit better. But how could this little boy with kind blue eyes be so violent?

'What if the pair of you tried to give up fighting?' said Mum. 'You can always *talk* things through instead, can't you? You know, Smidge, there isn't a single thing that can't be sorted out by talking it over properly.'

'Oh yes there is,' said Smidge. 'Take yesterday. I had to fight Kris then, too.'

'There was absolutely no need to,' said Mum. 'You could just as well have decided who was right by having a sensible discussion.'

Smidge sat down at the kitchen table and rested his battered head in his hands.

'So you say,' he said, glaring at his mother,

'but Kris said: "I can beat you up," and then I said: "Oh no you can't." How could a sensible discussion have sorted that out, eh?'

Mum had no answer, and her peace lecture came to a sudden end. Her fighter son looked rather down in the dumps, so she quickly put some hot chocolate and fresh buns on the table in front of him. That was something Smidge really liked. He had smelt the lovely, sweet smell of fresh baking as he was coming up the stairs, and Mum's delicious cinnamon buns at least made life a bit easier to cope with. Smidge sank his teeth thoughtfully into a bun, and while he was eating Mum put a plaster on the bump on his forehead. Then she gave the plaster a light kiss and asked:

'What did you and Kris fall out about today, then?'

'Kris and Jemima say Karlsson is an invention. They say he's just something I made up,' said Smidge.

'Well, isn't he?' asked Mum cautiously.

Smidge glared at her resentfully over his cup of chocolate.

'Can't *you* believe what I say, at least?' he said.

'I've asked Karlsson if he's just an invention . . . '

'And what did Karlsson say to that?' asked Mum. 'He said that if he *had* been an invention, he would have been the best invention in the world. But it so happens he isn't one,' said Smidge, taking another bun. 'Karlsson thinks it's Kris and Jemima who are inventions. Particularly dim-witted inventions, he says, and I think so too.'

Mum didn't answer. She realized it was pointless trying to get anywhere with Smidge's fantasies, so all she said was:

'I think you should play with Kris and Jemima a bit more, and not think about Karlsson so much.'

'At least Karlsson doesn't hurl boulders at me,' said Smidge, fingering the bump on his forehead. Then a thought occurred to him, and he gave Mum a sunny smile.

'By the way, I'm going to go and see where Karlsson lives today,' he said. 'I'd almost forgotten.'

He regretted it as soon as he'd said it. How could he be so stupid as to tell Mum?

But it didn't sound any more risky or worrying to Mum than anything else he had told her about Karlsson, and she said vaguely, 'Oh well, that will be fun for you.'

She wouldn't have been quite so calm if she'd actually concentrated on what Smidge was saying. And thought about exactly where Karlsson lived!

Smidge got up from the table, full and happy and suddenly very content with his world. The bump on his head didn't hurt any more, he still had the delicious taste of cinnamon bun in his mouth, the sun was shining in through the kitchen window, and Mum looked so nice with her round arms and checked apron. He gave her a short, hard hug and said:

'I do like you, Mum.'

'I'm glad about that,' said Mum.

'Yes . . . I like you because of all the nice things about you.'

Then he went to his room and sat down to wait for Karlsson. He would be going up onto the roof with him—what did it matter then that Kris said Karlsson was just an invention?

Smidge had a long wait.

'I'll be there about three or four or five o'clock,

but not a minute before six,' Karlsson had said.

Smidge wasn't really clear about when Karlsson was planning to come, so he asked again.

'No later than seven, anyway,' Karlsson said. 'But hardly before eight. And make sure you're ready at nine o'clock or roughly thereabouts, because that's when it all happens!'

Smidge felt as if he was waiting for ever, and in the end he decided Karlsson must have gone and turned into an invention and that was that. But all at once he heard the usual whirr, and in came Karlsson, bright and cheery.

'I've been waiting for ages,' said Smidge. 'When did you say you were coming?'

'*Roughly*,' said Karlsson. 'I said I'd be coming roughly, and so I have.'

He went over to Smidge's fish tank, thrust his whole face into the water and drank big gulps of it.

'Hey, mind my fish,' said Smidge anxiously. He was afraid Karlsson would swallow some of the little guppies swimming merrily round in the tank.

'When you've got a temperature, you have to keep drinking like mad,' said Karlsson. 'And if

a little fish or two slips down by mistake, that's
a mere trifle.'

'Have you got a temperature?' asked Smidge.

'I should say I have! Feel here,' said Karlsson,
putting Smidge's hand on his brow.

But Karlsson didn't feel particularly hot to
Smidge. 'How high is it, your temperature?'
he asked. 'Well, thirty or forty degrees,' said
Karlsson. 'At least!'

Smidge had recently had measles, and he

knew what having a temperature felt like. He shook his head.

'I don't think you're ill,' he said.

'You're a disgrace,' said Karlsson, and stamped his foot. 'Aren't I *ever* allowed to be ill like other people?'

'Do you want to be ill?' asked Smidge in surprise.

'Everybody wants to be, don't they?' said Karlsson. 'I want to lie in my bed with a raging, raging temperature, and you'll ask how I am and I'll say I'm the illest in the world, and you'll ask if there's anything I want, and I'll say that I feel so ill, so ill, that I don't want anything . . . except lots of cake and plenty of biscuits, and oodles of chocolate and a whole pile of sweets.'

Karlsson looked expectantly at Smidge, who was standing there at a loss, not knowing where he was suddenly supposed to get hold of all the things Karlsson wanted.

'I want you to be like a mother to me,' Karlsson went on, 'and you'll say I've got to take some nasty medicine . . . But then you'll give me five öre. Then you'll wrap a warm scarf round my neck, and I'll say it itches . . . Unless you give me another five öre.'

Smidge very much wanted to be like a mother to Karlsson. And that meant he had to empty his piggy bank. It stood on the bookcase, splendidly heavy. Smidge fetched a knife from the kitchen and set about prising out some five öre coins. Karlsson helped him with great enthusiasm and cheered as each coin came tumbling out. There were some ten öre and twenty-five öre coins too, but Karlsson liked the fives best.

Then Smidge ran down to the sweet shop and spent almost all his money on sweets and chocolates. As he handed over his money, he thought for a moment about how he had been saving it all up to buy a dog. The thought made him sigh a little. But he could see that anyone who had to be like a mother to Karlsson wouldn't be able to afford to keep a dog.

Smidge took a little detour through the sitting room on the way back, with the collection of sweets well hidden in his trouser pockets. They were all sitting there, Mum and Dad and Seb and Sally, having their after-dinner coffee. But today Smidge hadn't got time to join them. For a moment he toyed with the idea of inviting them in to meet Karlsson, but on further thought he decided not to. They would only stop him going up onto the roof with Karlsson. It would be much better for them to meet him another day.

Smidge took a couple of almond cookies from the coffee tray—because, after all, Karlsson had said he wanted biscuits, too—and then hurried back to his room.

'How long am I expected to sit here waiting, all ill and miserable like this?' Karlsson asked reproachfully. 'My temperature's rising several degrees a minute; you could boil eggs on me now.'

'I went as fast as I could,' said Smidge. 'And I bought so much . . . '

'But I hope you've still got some money left, so you can give me five öre when the scarf itches,' said Karlsson anxiously.

Smidge reassured him. He had kept back a few five öre pieces.

Karlsson's eyes shone, and he jumped for joy.

'Oh, I'm the illest in the world,' he said. 'We'd better hurry up and get me to bed.'

Only now did Smidge start to wonder how he was going to get up onto the roof, since he couldn't fly.

'Easy now, take it easy,' said Karlsson. 'I'll put you on my back and, heysan hopsan, we'll fly up to my place! Just make sure you don't get your fingers caught in the propeller.'

'But do you really think you can carry me?' asked Smidge.

'We'll soon find out,' said Karlsson. 'It'll be quite interesting to see if I manage to get further than halfway, while I'm all ill and miserable like this. But there's always the option of tipping you off, if I find I can't manage.'

Smidge didn't think being tipped off halfway up to the roof sounded a very good option, and looked a little wary.

'It'll be fine, I'm sure,' said Karlsson. 'Just as long as my motor doesn't stall.'

'But if it does, we'll crash,' said Smidge.

'Splat, we certainly will,' said Karlsson cheerfully. 'But that's a mere trifle,' he said, flicking his fingers.

Smidge decided to think it was a mere trifle, too.

He wrote a little note to Mum and Dad and put it on the table.

It would be best if he had time to get back before they saw the note. But if they happened to miss him, they would need to know where he was. Otherwise there might be the same fuss as that time at Granny's, when Smidge took it into his head to go on the train by himself. Mum cried afterwards and said, 'Oh, Smidge, if you wanted to go on the train, why didn't you tell me?'

'Because I *wanted* to go on the train,' said Smidge. It was the same thing now. He *wanted* to go up to the roof with Karlsson, and that meant the best thing was not to tell anyone. If they discovered he was gone, he could always argue that at least he had written that note.

Karlsson was ready to go. He turned the winder on his tummy, and his motor started to whirr.

'Jump on,' he said. 'We're off!'

And off they went. Out through the window and up into the air. Karlsson did an extra circuit over the top of the nearest buildings to check his motor was working properly. And it was chugging away so smoothly and evenly that

Smidge wasn't the least scared, and found he was enjoying himself.

Finally, Karlsson landed on their own roof.

'Now let's see if you can find my house,' said Karlsson. 'I'm not going to tell you it's behind the chimney, you'll have to work that out for yourself.'

Smidge had never been up on a roof before. But sometimes he'd seen men clearing snow, walking about on roofs with ropes tied round their waists. Smidge had always thought they were lucky to be able to do that. But now he was just as lucky himself—though he hadn't got a rope round his waist, of course, and he had such butterflies in his tummy as he balanced his way along to the chimney. Sure enough, there behind it lay Karlsson's little house. Oh, it was so sweet, with green shutters and a nice set of front steps to sit on if you wanted. But right now, Smidge just wanted to get inside the house as soon as possible and see all the steam engines and cockerel paintings and everything else Karlsson had.

There was a sign over the door so you knew who lived there.

the sign said.

And Karlsson flung the door open wide and shouted:

'Welcome, my dear Karlsson . . . and you too, Smidge!'

Then he rushed in first, in front of Smidge.

'I've got to get to bed, because I'm the illest in the world,' he shouted, and dived head first onto a redpainted, rib-backed settee against one of the walls.

Smidge followed him in. He was so curious he thought he might go pop.

It was jolly nice at Karlsson's, Smidge could see that at once. Apart from the settee there was a carpentry bench, which Karlsson obviously also used as a table, and then a cupboard and a couple of chairs and an open fire with an iron grating over it. That must be where Karlsson did his cooking.

But there were no steam engines to be seen. Smidge took his time looking round, but couldn't spot a single one, and in the end he had to ask:

'Where do you keep your steam engines?'

'Hrrm,' said Karlsson. 'My steam engines . . . they all exploded. Faulty safety valves, the lot of them! But that's a mere trifle and nothing to be glum about.'

Smidge looked all round again.

'What about your cockerel pictures, then, did they explode too?' he asked sarcastically.

'They most certainly did not,' said Karlsson. 'What do you think that is?' he asked, pointing to a piece of card pinned on the wall next to the cupboard. Right down in one corner of the card there really was a cockerel, a tiny red cockerel. Apart from that, the piece of card was blank.

'"A very lonely cockerel", that picture's called,' said Karlsson.

Smidge looked at the little cockerel. Karlsson's thousand cockerel pictures—was this pathetic little bird all there was, when it came to it?

'Very lonely cockerel, painted by the world's best cockerel painter,' said Karlsson, his voice trembling. 'Oh, how beautiful and sad that picture is! But I mustn't start crying, or my temperature will go even higher.'

He threw himself back against his pillows and put his hand to his forehead.

'You're supposed to be like a mother to me, so get started,' he said.

Smidge didn't know quite how to begin.

'Have you got any medicine?' he said dubiously.

'Yes, but none I want to take,' said Karlsson. 'Have you got five öre?'

Smidge fished a coin out of his trouser pocket.

'Give me that first,' said Karlsson. Smidge gave him the coin. Karlsson gripped it tightly in his hand, looking very sly and pleased with himself.

'I know what sort of medicine I can take,' he said.

'What sort, then?' asked Smidge.

'Karlsson on the Roof's cock-a-doodle-moo medicine. It's half sweets and half chocolate, all stirred up with some bits of biscuit. You get some ready, then I can take a dose straight away,' said Karlsson. 'It helps bring your temperature down.'

'I don't believe you,' said Smidge.

'Let's bet on it,' said Karlsson. 'I bet you a

bar of chocolate I'm right.'

Smidge thought maybe this was what Mum meant when she said you could decide who was right by having a sensible discussion.

'Shall we bet on it?' asked Karlsson again.

'Go on then,' said Smidge.

He got out the two bars of chocolate he'd bought and put them on the carpentry bench, so they could see what was at stake. Then he mixed up some medicine, using Karlsson's recipe. He took some acid drops and raspberry jelly sweets and toffees, and mixed them in a cup with the same number of squares of chocolate, and then he crumbled the almond cookies and sprinkled them on top. Smidge had never seen a medicine like it in his life, but it looked very tempting, and he almost wished he had a temperature of his own so he could try it, too.

But Karlsson sat there in bed, opening his beak as wide as a baby bird, and Smidge quickly found a spoon.

'Pour a good, big dose down me,' said Karlsson.

So that was what Smidge did.

Then they both sat still, waiting for Karlsson's temperature to come down.

After half a minute, Karlsson said, 'You're right. It hasn't helped. I've still got a temperature. Give me the bar of chocolate!'

'Give *you* the chocolate?' said Smidge in surprise. 'But I won.'

'Since you won, it surely isn't asking too much for me to get the chocolate?' said Karlsson. 'There has to be some justice in the world. What's more, you're a horrid little boy, sitting there expecting chocolate just because *I've* got a temperature.'

Smidge reluctantly passed the bar of chocolate to Karlsson. Karlsson immediately sank his teeth into it, and said as he chewed, 'No sour faces, thank you. Next time I'll win and *you'll* get the bar of chocolate.'

He chomped away with relish, and when he had finished the very last bite he lay back on his pillows and gave a heavy sigh.

'I feel so sorry for everyone who's ill,' he said. 'I feel so sorry for me! I suppose we could always try a double dose of the cock-a-doodle-moo medicine, but I don't believe for a minute it'll work.'

'Oh yes, I think a double dose should do the

trick,' Smidge said quickly. 'Shall we have a bet on it?'

Smidge could be cunning, too, you see. He was convinced even a triple dose of cock-a-doodle-moo medicine wouldn't cure Karlsson's high temperature, but he did very much want to lose a bet. Because he only had one bar of chocolate left, and he would get to keep it if Karlsson won the bet.

'A bet, that's fine by me,' said Karlsson. 'Mix up a double dose! Where temperatures are concerned, you have to try simply everything. All we can do is test it and see.'

Smidge mixed up a double dose of the medicine and stuffed it into Karlsson, who gladly opened wide and swallowed it down.

Then they sat still and waited. After half a minute, Karlsson leapt out of bed, beaming with delight.

'It's a miracle,' he shouted. 'My temperature's normal. You've won again. Pass me the bar of chocolate!'

Smidge sighed and handed over his last bar of chocolate. Karlsson gave him a disapproving look.

'Moody brutes like you should never make bets,' he said. 'It's all right for folk like me, who go about like little sunbeams whether we win or lose.'

There was silence for a moment, apart from the smacking of Karlsson's lips as he gorged on the chocolate. Then he said:

'But since you're a greedy little boy, I suppose we'd better share the rest in a brotherly fashion—have you got any sweets left?'

Smidge felt in his pocket.

'Three,' he said, pulling out two toffees and a raspberry jelly sweet.

'Three,' said Karlsson, 'you can't divide those equally, even the littlest child knows that.'

He took the raspberry jelly sweet from Smidge's outstretched hand and gobbled it up.

'But *now* you can,' he said.

Then he eyed the two toffees hungrily. One was a little bit bigger than the other.

'Since I'm so good-natured, I shall let you choose first,' said Karlsson. 'But you do know, don't you, that the one who chooses first has to take the smaller toffee?' he went on, looking sternly at Smidge.

Smidge thought about it for a minute and had a good idea.

'I want you to choose first,' he said.

'All right, if you insist,' said Karlsson, and grabbed the biggest toffee, which he stuffed straight into his mouth.

Smidge looked at the little toffee still lying in his hand.

'Hey, I thought you said the one who chose first had to take the smallest . . .'

'Now listen here, you little greedy little pig,' said Karlsson. 'If you'd got to choose first, which one would you have taken?'

'I'd have taken the smallest one, really I would,' said Smidge earnestly.

'So what are you making a fuss about?' asked Karlsson. 'You jolly well got the one you wanted.'

Smidge wondered again, if this was the sort of thing Mum meant by 'a sensible discussion'.

But Smidge never stayed in a bad mood for long. It was good news, after all, that Karlsson hadn't got a temperature any more. Karlsson thought so too.

'I shall write to all the doctors and tell them

the cure for a high temperature. "Try Karlsson on the Roof's cock-a-doodle-moo medicine," I shall write, "the world's best high temperature cure!"'

Smidge still hadn't eaten up his toffee. It looked so wonderfully chewy and delicious that he wanted to admire it for a while first. Once he started eating it, it would all be nearly over.

Karlsson was looking at Smidge's toffee as well. He looked at Smidge's toffee for a long time, put his head on one side and said, 'Shall we make a bet that I can make your toffee disappear by magic, without you seeing?'

'Oh, you won't be able to,' said Smidge. 'Not if I stand here holding it in my hand and look at it the whole time.'

'Let's bet on it,' said Karlsson.

'No,' said Smidge. 'I know I shall win, and then you'll get the toffee . . . '

Smidge knew this was the wrong way to decide a bet, because it never worked like this when he made bets with Seb or Sally.

'But we can make a bet the ordinary, proper way, so the one who *wins* gets the toffee,' said Smidge.

'Whatever you like, you greedy little boy,'

said Karlsson. 'Let's bet I can make the toffee disappear by magic, without you seeing it.'

'Go on then,' said Smidge.

'Hocus pocus filiocus,' said Karlsson, and grabbed the toffee. 'Hocus pocus filiocus,' he said, and popped it in his mouth.

'Stop!' shouted Smidge. 'I *did* see you making it disappear . . .'

'Oh, did you?' said Karlsson, swallowing quickly. 'Well then, you've won again. I've never known a boy win so many bets.'

'Yes . . . but . . . the toffee . . . ' said Smidge, totally confused. 'The one who won was supposed to get the toffee.'

'Yes, that's true,' said Karlsson, 'but I've made the toffee disappear by magic, and I bet you I can't make it come back.'

Smidge said nothing. But he was thinking that as soon as he saw Mum, he would tell her sensible discussions were no use at all for deciding who was right.

He felt in his empty trouser pocket. And guess what, there was another toffee that he hadn't noticed before! A lovely, big, chewy toffee. Smidge laughed.

'I bet you I've got another toffee,' he said. 'And I bet you I'm going to eat it straight up,' he said, and popped the toffee swiftly into his mouth.

Karlsson sat down on the bed, looking sulky.

'You were supposed to be like a mother to me,' he said. 'But instead, all you're doing is stuffing yourself. I've never seen such a greedy little boy.'

He sat in silence for a while, looking even more dejected.

'And by the way, I never did get that five öre for wearing the itchy scarf,' he said.

'No, but then you haven't been wearing a scarf,' said Smidge.

'There isn't a single scarf in the whole house,' said Karlsson peevishly. 'But if there had been, I would have worn it, and then it would have itched, and I would have got five öre.'

He looked imploringly at Smidge, and his eyes were full of tears.

'Should I be made to suffer because there isn't a scarf in the house, do you think?'

Smidge didn't think he should. So he gave Karlsson on the Roof his last five öre coin.

Karlsson Gets
up to Some
Jiggery-pokery

'Right, I'm in the mood for a bit of fun now,' said Karlsson a little while later. 'Let's take a walk on the rooftops round about, and I'm sure we'll come up with something.'

Smidge was more than happy with the idea. He took Karlsson's hand, and together they marched out of the door and onto the roof. It would soon be getting dark, and everything looked so beautiful. The air was that special blue it sometimes is in spring; all the houses looked mysterious and exciting, the way houses do at dusk; the park where Smidge often played was gleaming wonderfully green, way down there, and the glorious scent of the big balsam poplar in the courtyard of the flats reached right up to the roof.

It was a wonderful evening for rooftop walks. All the windows were open, and you could hear so many different sounds. People talking, children laughing and children crying. There was the clatter of crockery from a nearby kitchen where somebody was washing up; a dog whimpering, and somewhere, someone was tinkling on a piano. From down in the street you could hear the pop-pop of a motorbike, and as that died away a carthorse came clopping along, pulling a cart, and every clop carried right up to the roof.

'If people knew how great it is walking on roofs, there'd be nobody left down there in the street,' said Smidge. 'It's such fun!'

'Yes, and thrilling too,' said Karlsson, 'because you can so easily slip off. I'll show you a few places where you're guaranteed to *almost* slip off every time.'

The buildings were so tightly packed together that you could step from one roof to the next. There were lots of odd little gable ends and attic rooms and chimneys and angles and corners, so it never got boring. And it really was thrilling, just like Karlsson said, precisely because you *almost* slipped every now and then. There was one place where the gap between two buildings was quite wide, and that was one of those places where Smidge nearly slipped off. But Karlsson caught him at the last minute, when one of Smidge's legs was already dangling over the edge of the roof.

'Fun, isn't it?' said Karlsson, hauling Smidge back up. 'That was just the sort of thing I meant. Do it again!' But Smidge didn't want to do it again. It was a bit too 'almost' for him. There were several places where you really had to cling on with your arms and your legs to stop yourself falling, and Karlsson wanted Smidge to enjoy himself as much as possible, so he didn't always take the easiest route.

'I think we'll try a bit of jiggery-pokery now,' said Karlsson. 'I usually take a turn about the roof of an evening and do a bit of jiggery-pokery for the people who live in all these attic rooms.'

'What do you do to them?' asked Smidge.

'I have different jiggery-pokes for different people, of course. Never the same one twice. The world's best jiggery-poker, guess who that is!'

Just then, a baby started screaming somewhere close by. Smidge had heard that child crying before, but then it had gone quiet for a while. The baby must have been having a little rest. But now it was starting up again, and the cries were coming from the nearest window in the roof. It sounded so pathetic and forlorn.

'Poor little thing,' said Smidge. 'Maybe it's got tummy ache.'

'We'll soon find out,' said Karlsson. 'Come on!' They climbed along the gutter until they were just under the window, and then Karlsson cautiously popped up his head and peered in.

'Very lonely baby,' he said. 'Mummy and Daddy are out gallivanting, I expect.'

The baby cried more pitifully than ever.

'Easy now, take it easy,' said Karlsson, pulling himself over the window ledge. 'Here comes

Karlsson on the Roof, the world's best nanny.'

Smidge didn't want to be left on his own outside. He wriggled over the window ledge after Karlsson, though he felt rather anxious about what might happen if the child's mum and dad suddenly came home.

But Karlsson wasn't the least anxious. He went over to the baby's cot and stuck a podgy finger under its chin.

'Goo goo ga ga,' he said roguishly. Then he turned to Smidge.

'That's what you say to babies; they like it.'

The baby stopped crying in sheer surprise, but as soon as it had recovered, it started again.

'Goo goo ga ga . . . and then you do this,' said Karlsson. He snatched the baby from its cot and hoisted it towards the ceiling, several times. Maybe the baby enjoyed it, because it suddenly smiled a little toothless smile.

Karlsson looked proud of himself.

'Nothing to it, this cheering up babies,' he said. 'The world's best nan—' That was as far as he got before the baby started crying again.

'Goo goo ga ga,' roared Karlsson angrily, hoisting the baby up into the air more roughly than before. 'Goo goo ga ga, I said, and I mean it!'

The baby screamed fit to burst, and Smidge held out his arms for it.

'Come on, let me hold her,' he said. He really liked tiny children, and he had argued quite a bit with Mum and Dad about whether he could have a little sister, since they stubbornly refused to let him have a dog.

He took the little bundle from Karlsson and held it tenderly in his arms.

'Please don't cry,' he said. The baby went quiet and looked at him with a pair of bright, serious eyes. Then it smiled its toothless smile again and burbled quietly.

'It's my goo goo ga ga that did the trick,' said Karlsson. 'That's one thing that never fails, I've put it to the test a thousand times.'

'I wonder what the baby's name is,' said Smidge, stroking his finger along her soft little cheek.

'Sweetie-Pie,' said Karlsson, 'that's what most of them are called.'

Smidge had never heard of a baby being called Sweetie-Pie, but he supposed the world's best nanny knew more about babies' names than he did.

'Little Sweetie-Pie,' said Smidge, 'I think you're hungry.'

Because Sweetie-Pie had grabbed hold of his finger and was trying to suck it.

'If Sweetie-Pie's hungry, there's some sausage and mash over here,' said Karlsson, looking into the tiny kitchen. 'No child need starve, as long as Karlsson has the strength to deliver the sausage and mash.'

Smidge didn't think Sweetie-Pie could eat sausage and mash.

'Babies this small are supposed to have milk, aren't they?' he said.

'Don't you think the world's best nanny knows what children can eat and what they can't?' said Karlsson. 'All right then, I'll fly off and find a cow!'

He cast an angry glance at the window.

'But it's going to be tricky getting the poor old cow through that poky little window.'

Sweetie-Pie was reaching desperately for Smidge's finger and whimpering miserably. She really did sound hungry.

Smidge checked the kitchen, but he couldn't find any milk. There were just three slices of cold sausage on a saucer.

'Easy now, take it easy,' said Karlsson. 'I've just remembered where there's some milk. I often have a slurp myself, when I'm passing. Heysan hopsan, I'll be back soon.'

Then Karlsson turned the winder on his tummy and whirred off through the window, before Smidge could bat an eyelid.

Smidge was dreadfully scared. What if Karlsson was gone for hours, like he usually was? And what if the baby's mum and dad came home and found Smidge with their Sweetie-Pie in his arms?

But Smidge didn't have long to worry. This time, Karlsson had hurried up. He buzzed in through the window like the cock of the walk, holding one of those feeding bottles babies use.

'Where did you get that?' asked Smidge, surprised. 'At my usual place for milk,' said Karlsson. 'A balcony in another part of town!'

'Did you *pinch* it?' asked Smidge in alarm.

'I happen to have borrowed it,' said Karlsson haughtily.

'Borrowed . . . When are you thinking of taking it back, then?' Smidge asked.

'Never,' said Karlsson.

Smidge gave him a stern look, but Karlsson flicked his fingers and said, 'One little bottle of milk—that's a mere trifle! The person I've borrowed this from has got triplets, and keeps loads and loads of bottles cool in ice buckets on their balcony, and they like me borrowing their milk for Sweetie-Pie.'

Sweetie-Pie stretched out her little hands for the bottle and squealed hungrily.

'I'll warm it up a bit,' said Smidge quickly, and passed Sweetie-Pie over to Karlsson, and Karlsson shouted *'goo goo ga ga'* and hoisted Sweetie-Pie up in the air, while Smidge went to the little kitchen to warm the bottle.

And a short while later, Sweetie-Pie lay sleeping like an angel in her cot. She was full and happy, Smidge had tucked her in, and Karlsson had prodded her with his finger and shouted *'goo goo ga ga'*, but Sweetie-Pie dozed off all the same, because she was so full and sleepy.

'We'll just do a bit of jiggery-pokery before we go,' said Karlsson.

He went into the kitchen and brought back the three slices of cold sausage. Smidge watched him wide-eyed.

'Now just you watch this for jiggery-pokery,' said Karlsson, hanging one slice of sausage on the handle of the kitchen door.

'Number one,' he announced, nodding with satisfaction. Then he went briskly over to the bureau. A lovely white china dove was standing on it, and before Smidge knew it, the white dove had a slice of sausage in its beak.

'Number two,' said Karlsson. 'And number three's for Sweetie-Pie.'

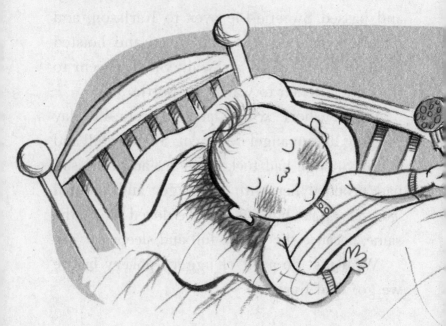

He skewered the last slice of sausage on a little stick and put the stick in the sleeping baby's hand. It looked very funny; you might almost believe Sweetie-Pie herself had been to the kitchen to fetch some sausage and then fallen asleep over it, but Smidge still felt he had to say:

'Oh don't do that, please!'

'Easy now, take it easy,' said Karlsson. 'That ought to put her mum and dad off gallivanting in the evenings.'

'How?' asked Smidge.

'They won't dare leave a baby who can walk and help herself to a sausage on her own any more. Because who knows what she might decide to take next time . . . Daddy's Sunday beer, maybe.'

He adjusted the stick so it was held more firmly in Sweetie-Pie's hand.

'Easy now, take it easy,' he said. 'I know what I'm doing, all right, because I'm the world's best nanny.'

Just then Smidge heard footsteps on the stairs, and almost jumped out of his skin with fright.

'Oh no, they're coming!' he whispered.

'Easy now, take it easy,' said Karlsson, and they both rushed to the window. Smidge heard a key being inserted in the lock, and he thought there was no chance, but somehow he managed to scramble over the window ledge. A second later he heard the door open and a voice said:

'Mummy's little Suzy, fast asleep.'

'Yes, fast asleep,' said another voice. Then there was a shriek. And Smidge knew Sweetie-Pie's mum and dad had seen the sausage.

He didn't wait to hear what happened next, *but* scurried to catch up with the world's best nanny, who was just hiding behind a chimney pot.

'Do you want to see a couple of thugs?' asked Karlsson, when they had had a little rest. 'I've got two first-class thugs in another attic over here.'

Karlsson almost made it sound as if they were his very own thugs. They couldn't be, of course, but Smidge wanted to see them all the same.

Voices and howls of laughter were coming from their window in the roof.

'Well well, they *are* in a good mood,' said Karlsson. 'Let's go and see what's amusing them so much.'

They crept along the gutter, and Karlsson popped his head up to look in. There were curtains across the window, but there was a gap in them for him to peep through.

'The thugs have got a visitor,' whispered Karlsson. Smidge peeped in, too. He saw two rough characters sitting there, who might very well be the thugs, and with them was a small, harmless, kindly looking man who looked as if he might come from the countryside, where

Granny lived.

'Do you know what?' whispered Karlsson. 'I reckon those thugs are trying a bit of jiggery-pokery for themselves. But they're going to have to stop.'

He looked in again.

'Sure as eggs is eggs, those thugs are jiggery-poking that poor chap with the red tie,' he whispered to Smidge.

The thugs and their guest with the red tie were sitting round a little table just under the window. They were eating and drinking, and the thugs were slapping the man with the red tie heartily on the back and saying, 'We're so glad we met you, dear Oskar!'

'I'm glad, too,' said Oskar. 'When you arrive in the city like I just have, you need some good friends, fellows you can rely on. Otherwise there's no knowing what might happen. You might get taken in by swindlers.'

The thugs nodded.

'Quite right, you might run into swindlers,' said one of them. 'What a good job you met Spike and me!'

'Yes, if you hadn't met Rollo and me, things

could have turned out very bad,' said the other one.

'Now you just eat and drink and enjoy yourself,' said the one called Spike, and slapped Oskar on the back again. Then he did something that amazed Smidge. As if by accident, he slipped his hand into Oskar's back pocket and took out his wallet, which he tucked carefully into the back pocket of his own trousers. And Oscar didn't notice a thing. Maybe because at that moment, Rollo was hanging round his neck and slapping his back. But when Rollo had finished his slapping and took his hand away, Oskar's watch just happened to come too. Rollo stuffed it in the back pocket of *his* trousers. And Oskar didn't notice a thing.

But then, Karlsson on the Roof cautiously reached in through the gap in the curtains with one chubby hand and took the wallet out of Spike's back pocket, and Spike didn't notice a thing. Then Karlsson reached in with one chubby hand and took the watch out of Rollo's back pocket, and Rollo didn't notice a thing.

A short while later, after Oskar and Rollo and Spike had had some more to eat and drink, Spike put his hand in his back pocket and discovered the wallet was missing. Then he glowered at Rollo and said:

'Listen here, Rollo, come out to the hall, there's something I need to talk to you about.'

Just then, Rollo felt in his back pocket and noticed the watch was missing. And he glowered at Spike and said:

'That suits me fine, because there's something I need to talk to you about, too.'

So Rollo and Spike went out into the hall, and poor Oskar was left sitting on his own. He soon got bored, and went out to the hall to see what was keeping Rollo and Spike. Then Karlsson clambered quickly over the window ledge and put Oskar's wallet in the soup tureen. But Rollo and Spike and Oskar had finished up the soup, so it didn't get wet. And Karlsson fixed Oskar's watch to the lamp above the table, where it dangled down and was the first thing Oskar and Rollo and Spike saw when they came back in. But they didn't see Karlsson, because he had crept under the tablecloth, which went right down to the floor. And by then, Smidge was also sitting under the table, because he wanted to be wherever Karlsson was, even if it was risky.

'Look, that's my watch hanging there,' said Oskar. 'How in the world did it get there?'

And he unhooked the watch and put it in his waistcoat pocket.

'And there's my wallet,' he said, staring down into the soup tureen. 'How very odd!'

Rollo and Spike looked admiringly at Oskar, and Spike said, 'Seems like you country folk aren't as slow as they say.'

Then Rollo and Spike and Oskar sat back down at the table.

'Oscar my friend, have some more to eat and drink,' said Spike.

And Oskar and Rollo and Spike ate and drank and slapped each other on the back. And a short while later, Spike's hand reached under the tablecloth and laid Oskar's wallet carefully on the floor. He thought it would be safer there than in his trouser pocket. But it wasn't, because Karlsson grabbed up the wallet straight away and passed it to Rollo, and Rollo took the wallet and said:

'Spike, I've done you an injustice; you're an

honest man.'

A short while later, Rollo's hand reached under the tablecloth and laid Oskar's watch carefully on the floor. Karlsson picked up the watch and gently shook Spike's leg and passed Oskar's watch to him, and Spike said:

'Nobody could have a better mate than you, Rollo.'

But a bit later, Oskar asked:

'Where's my wallet? And where's my watch?'

And then the wallet and the watch were both popped under the tablecloth as quick as a flash, because Spike didn't dare keep the watch and Rollo didn't dare keep the wallet, if Oskar was going to start making a fuss. And Oskar certainly did start making a fuss, quite a loud one, shouting that he wanted his watch and his wallet, but then Spike said:

'How are we supposed to know where you've gone and left your old wallet?'

And Rollo said:

'We haven't seen your old watch; keep a better eye on your things!'

But then Karlsson picked up first the wallet and then the watch, and passed them up to

Oskar, who put them both away and said:

'Thank you, Spike, and thank you, Rollo. But that's quite enough joking for now.'

Then Karlsson kicked Spike's shin as hard as he could, and Spike roared:

'I'll get you for that, Rollo!'

Then Karlsson kicked Rollo's shin as hard as he could, and Rollo roared:

'What's up with you, Spike, why are you kicking me?'

And Rollo and Spike leapt up and hurled themselves at each other, knocking all the plates off the table and smashing them. Oskar was so scared that he crept out with his wallet and watch and never came back.

Smidge was scared too, but he couldn't leave, so he had to sit quiet and still under the tablecloth.

Spike was stronger than Rollo, and he chased Rollo out into the hall and stayed to beat him up a bit more. Then Karlsson and Smidge crawled out from under the tablecloth and saw all the smashed plates on the floor, and Karlsson said, 'Why should the soup tureen be left in one piece, when all the plates are broken? It'll be so lonely, poor soup tureen!'

So he hurled the tureen onto the floor with a crash, and then he and Smidge raced to the window and climbed out as fast as they could. Smidge heard Spike and Rollo come back into the room, and Spike said, 'Why on earth did you give him back his watch and wallet, fishface?'

'Are you off your head?' said Rollo. '*You* were

the one who did it.'

That made Karlsson laugh until his belly wobbled, and then he said, 'That's enough jiggery-pokery for me today.'

Smidge felt he had had enough jiggery-pokery, too.

It was getting quite dark, and Smidge and Karlsson took each other by the hand and walked back over the roofs to Karlsson's house, which was on top of Smidge's house. As they got back they heard a fire engine coming along the street with its siren wailing.

'There must be a fire somewhere,' said Smidge. 'The fire brigade's coming.'

'What if it's in this building?' said Karlsson hopefully. 'They only need to say the word, and I can help them, because I'm the world's best fire putter-outer.'

They could see the fire engine had stopped in the street just below, and a crowd of people had gathered round it. But they couldn't see a fire anywhere. On the other hand, they did suddenly see a ladder come shooting up towards the roof, one of those turntable ladders the fire brigade use.

That made Smidge start to think.

'What if . . . What if . . . they're coming for *me*?' he said.

He had suddenly remembered the note he had left in his room. And it was getting quite late.

'Bless me, why ever would they do that?' said Karlsson. 'Nobody could mind you being up on the roof for a while.'

'Oh, my mum could,' said Smidge. 'She's got so many nerves that they fray in all directions.'

He felt sorry for Mum, when he thought about it, and longed to see her.

'We could have a bit of a jiggery-poke with the fire brigade, of course,' suggested Karlsson.

But Smidge didn't want to jiggery-poke any more. He stood quietly waiting for the firefighter who was climbing up the ladder.

'Oh well,' said Karlsson, 'perhaps it's time for me to pop indoors to bed. I know we've been taking it easy and not jiggery-poking too much, but I did have a temperature of at least thirty or forty degrees this morning, we must bear that in mind.'

And he scampered off over the roof.

'Heysan hopsan, Smidge,' he shouted.

'Heysan hopsan, Karlsson,' said Smidge.

But all the while he was watching the firefighter getting closer.

'Hey, Smidge,' called Karlsson, just before he vanished behind the chimney, 'don't tell the fire brigade I'm here. Because I'm the world's best fire putter-outer, and they'd only be asking for me, every time there was a fire.'

The firefighter was almost at roof level.

'Stay where you are,' he shouted to Smidge. 'Don't move, and I'll be right there to get you.'

It was kind of him, Smidge thought, but rather unnecessary. Smidge had been walking around on the roof all afternoon, so he could easily manage a few steps more. 'Was it my mum who sent you?' he asked, when he was on his way down the turntable ladder in the firefighter's arms.

'Yes, who else?' said the firefighter. 'But hang on a minute . . . didn't I see *two* little boys up on the roof . . . ?

Smidge remembered what Karlsson had told him, and answered earnestly, 'No, the only *boy* was *me*.'

Mum certainly did have enough nerves to fray in all directions. She and Dad and Seb and Sally and lots of other people were down in the street to receive Smidge. And Mum threw herself at him and hugged him, laughing and crying at the same time. And Dad carried him right up to the flat, cuddling him tightly all the way. And Seb said, 'You really know how to scare the daylights out of people, little brother.'

And Sally was crying too, and she said, 'You mustn't do that ever again, promise?'

And when Smidge was in bed a little while later, they all gathered round him as if it was his birthday. But Dad said very seriously, 'Didn't you realize we'd be worried? Didn't you realize Mum would cry and be upset?'

Smidge squirmed as he lay there.

'Not as upset as *that*,' he mumbled.

Mum hugged him really hard and said, 'What if you'd fallen? What if we'd lost you?'

'Would you all have been sad?' asked Smidge hopefully.

'Yes, of course,' said Mum. 'We wouldn't want to lose you at any price, surely you know that?'

'Not even for a hundred thousand million kronor?' asked Smidge.

'No, not even for a hundred thousand million kronor.'

'Am I worth that much?' asked Smidge in amazement.

'Oh yes,' said Mum, and hugged him again.

Smidge started thinking. A hundred thousand million kronor, what a terrible lot of money! Could it really be possible he was worth that much? When you could get a puppy, a really nice puppy, for two hundred kronor?

'You know what, Dad,' said Smidge, when he had finished thinking. 'If I'm worth a hundred thousand million kronor—could I please have two hundred of it in cash, so I can buy a little dog?'

Karlsson Plays Ghost

I t wasn't until they were at the dinner table the next day that they started asking Smidge how he got up on the roof.

'Did you climb out through the trapdoor in the attic?' asked Mum.

'No, I *flew* up with Karlsson on the Roof,' said Smidge.

Mum and Dad looked at each other.

'Now look, this has got to stop,' said Mum. 'This Karlsson on the Roof is driving me crazy.'

'Smidge, Karlsson on the Roof doesn't *exist*,' said Dad.

'Oh doesn't he?' said Smidge. 'Well, he was

there yesterday.'

Mum shook her head.

'It's a good job you break up from school soon, so you can go to Granny's,' she said. 'I hope Karlsson isn't thinking of going with you.'

That was a problem Smidge had overlooked. He would be at Granny's for the summer holidays and not see Karlsson for two months. It wasn't that he didn't like it at Granny's, he always really enjoyed himself there, but how he would miss Karlsson! And what if Karlsson wasn't living on the roof any longer by the time Smidge got back?

With his elbows on the table and his head resting in his hands, he tried to imagine what life would be like without Karlsson.

'No elbows on the table, you know the rules,' said Sally.

'Mind your own business,' said Smidge.

'No elbows on the table, Smidge,' said Mum. 'Would you like some more cauliflower?'

'No, I'd rather die,' said Smidge.

'Tsk, Smidge, that's not what you say,' said Dad. 'You say "No thank you".'

They had a bit of a cheek, bossing a hundred thousand million kronor boy about like that, thought Smidge, but he didn't say so. Instead he said, 'But if I say "I'd rather die," you know I mean "No thank you", anyway.'

'But a gentleman doesn't say that sort of thing,' Dad persisted. 'And you do *want* to be a gentleman, don't you, Smidge?'

'No, I want to be like you, Dad.'

Mum and Seb and Sally laughed. Smidge didn't understand why, but he had the feeling they were laughing at his dad, and he didn't like that.

'I want to be like Dad, who's so nice and kind,' he said, with a tender look at his father.

'Thank you,' said Dad. 'Now then, are you sure you don't want any more cauliflower?'

'No, I'd rather die,' said Smidge.

'But it's good for you,' said Mum.

'I thought so,' said Smidge. 'The worse you like a food, the better it turns out to be for you. Why do they have to put all the vitamins in stuff that tastes horrible, that's what I'd like to know.'

'Yes, funny that,' said Seb. 'I suppose you think they should be in toffee and chewing gum instead?'

'That's the most sensible thing you've said for a long time,' said Smidge.

After dinner, he went to his room. He hoped with all his heart that Karlsson would come. Smidge would be going away soon, after all, and he wanted to be with Karlsson as much as he could before then.

Maybe Karlsson could sense it, because he came flying along as soon as Smidge stuck his nose out of the window.

'No temperature today?' asked Smidge.

'Temperature . . . me?' exclaimed Karlsson. 'I never had a temperature. It was just imagination.'

'You just imagined you had a temperature?' asked Smidge in surprise.

'No, but I made you imagine I had,' said Karlsson with a self-satisfied chuckle. 'The world's best jiggerypoker, guess who that is?'

Karlsson couldn't keep still for a second. The whole time he was talking, he went twirling round the room, fingering things in his nosy way, opening all the drawers and cupboards he found and going through everything with great interest.

'No, I haven't got a temperature today,' he said. 'Today I'm on super-good form, and in the mood for a bit of fun.'

Smidge was in the mood for a bit of fun, too. But before all that he wanted Mum and Dad and Seb and Sally to see Karlsson, so he didn't have to keep hearing them say Karlsson didn't exist.

'Wait a tick,' he said quickly. 'I'll be straight back.'

He raced off to the sitting room. Seb and Sally had just gone out, annoyingly enough, but Mum and Dad were there at any rate, and Smidge said eagerly, 'Mum and Dad, please will you come to my room right now?'

He dared not mention Karlsson; it would be better for them to see him without any warning.

'Why not come and sit with us instead,' said Mum. But Smidge tugged at her arm.

'No, I want you to see something in my room.' After a bit of persuasion, they both agreed to come, and Smidge felt very happy as he threw open his bedroom door. Now they would see at last!

He could have cried with disappointment.

The room was empty—just like the last time he tried to show them Karlsson.

'What was it you wanted us to see?' asked Dad.

'Oh, nothing,' mumbled Smidge.

At that moment, luckily, the phone rang, so Smidge didn't have to explain. Dad went to answer it. Mum had a sponge cake in the oven that needed checking. Smidge was left on his own. He sat by the window feeling really cross with Karlsson, and decided to tell him a few home truths if he came flying by.

But nobody came flying by. Instead, the wardrobe door opened and Karlsson poked his cheery face out.

Smidge was taken totally by surprise.

'What on earth were you doing in my wardrobe?' he said.

'Hatching eggs . . . no! Sitting thinking about my sins . . . no! Lying on the shelf for a rest . . . yes!' said Karlsson.

Smidge forgot about being cross. He was just glad to have found Karlsson again.

'That's a great wardrobe for playing hide and seek in,' said Karlsson. 'Let's do it! I'll lie back down on the shelf, and you try to find me.'

Before Smidge could answer, Karlsson had vanished into the wardrobe, and Smidge could hear him climbing up onto the shelf.

'Start looking!' shouted Karlsson.

Smidge opened the wardrobe door wide and didn't have much trouble finding Karlsson up on the shelf.

'Shame on you, you mean boy!' shrieked Karlsson. 'You could at least have looked in the bed and behind the table and in other places *first*. Count me out if this is your way of doing it; I can't believe you're so mean!'

There came a ring at the front door, and a moment later Mum called from the hall.

'Smidge, Kris and Jemima are here.'

That was all it took to put Karlsson back in a good mood.

'We'll jiggery-poke them,' he whispered to Smidge. 'Shut the door on me!'

Smidge closed the wardrobe door, and the minute he'd done it, Jemima and Kris came in. They lived in the same road and were in Smidge's class at school. Smidge liked Jemima a lot, and often talked to his mum about how 'sweet' she was. He liked Kris, too, and had already forgiven him for that bump on his head. He and Kris quite often had fights, but afterwards they were just as good friends as ever. Anyway, it wasn't only Kris Smidge got into fights with; he had fought wild battles with nearly all the kids in the road. But he never touched Jemima.

'How is it you never come to blows with Jemima?' his mum once asked.

'Well, she's sweet, so I don't need to,' said Smidge.

But Jemima could be annoying sometimes, too, of course. Yesterday when they were coming home from school, Smidge had been talking about Karlsson, and Jemima had laughed and said Karlsson was just an invention and something he'd made up. And Kris had sided with her, so Smidge had had to wallop him, and that was when Kris threw the stone at Smidge's head.

But now they were here, and Kris had Woof with him. With Woof there, Smidge even forgot Karlsson, lying on the wardrobe shelf. Dogs were the nicest things in the world,

Smidge thought. Woof jumped about, barking, and Smidge put his arm round his neck and patted him. Kris stood watching, not the least worried. He knew, you see, that Woof was *his* dog and nobody else's, so Smidge was welcome to pat him as much as he liked.

While Smidge was busy patting Woof, Jemima said with an irritating snigger, 'So where's your old Karlsson on the Roof, then? We thought he'd be here.'

That was when Smidge remembered Karlsson was lying on the wardrobe shelf. But since he didn't know what sort of jiggery-pokery Karlsson was planning this time, he couldn't tell them. So he just said, 'Huh, you always say Karlsson on the Roof is something I've made up. You said yesterday he was just an invention.'

'Well he is,' said Jemima, laughing so the dimples in her cheeks showed.

'What if he isn't?' said Smidge.

'But he is,' said Kris.

'Oh no he isn't,' said Smidge.

He wondered whether there was any point carrying on with this 'sensible discussion' or whether he'd be better off punching Kris straight away. But before he could make his mind up, a loud 'Cock-a-doodle-doo' sound came from the wardrobe.

'What was *that*?' asked Jemima, and her mouth, which was small and red like a cherry, opened wide in amazement.

'Cock-a-doodle-doo,' they heard again, and it sounded just like a real cockerel.

'Is that a cockerel you've got in your wardrobe?' said Kris in surprise. But Smidge just laughed. He was laughing so much, he couldn't say a word.

'Cock-a-doodle-doo,' crowed the voice in the wardrobe.

'I'm going to open it and see,' said Jemima.

She opened the door and looked inside. Kris rushed over and looked inside as well. At first all they could see were loads of clothes hanging there. But then they heard a giggle coming from above their heads, and when they looked up they saw a little fat man lying on the shelf. He was propped comfortably on one elbow, one podgy leg dangling over the edge of the shelf, and his merry blue eyes were shining brightly.

Neither Jemima nor Kris said a word to start with, though Woof growled. But when Jemima found her tongue, she asked, 'Who's *that*?'

'Just a little invention,' said the strange figure up on the shelf, swinging his leg. 'A little invention, simply having a rest. In short . . . something made up!'

'Are you . . . are you . . . ?' stammered Kris.

'A little something Smidge made up, simply

lying here crowing, that's right,' said the little man.

'Are you Karlsson on the Roof?' whispered Jemima.

'Yes, of course,' said Karlsson. 'Did you think I was old Mrs Gustafson from number ninety-two, come in here for a quick lie down?'

Smidge could only laugh, because Jemima and Kris were standing there with their mouths wide open, looking stupid.

'That shut the pair of you up,' he said at last.

Karlsson hopped down from the shelf. He went over to Jemima and gave her cheek a mischievous tweak.

'What childish little invention do we have here, then?' he said.

'We . . . ' began Kris.

'What else are you called apart from Angus?' asked Karlsson.

'I'm not called Angus,' said Kris.

'Good, you carry on with that,' said Karlsson.

'They're called Jemima and Kris,' said Smidge.

'It's amazing what can happen to people,' said Karlsson. 'But don't let it get you down . . . I'm afraid we can't all be called Karlsson.'

He looked around in his nosy way and went on, without stopping for breath:

'I'm in the mood for a bit of fun. Can't we throw all the chairs out of the window or something?'

Smidge didn't think that was a very good idea, and he was sure Mum and Dad wouldn't either.

'Well, if they're old-fashioned, they're old-fashioned, and that's that,' said Karlsson. 'It can't be helped. In that case we'll have to think of something else, because I must have some fun. You can count me out, otherwise,' he said, pursing his mouth in a sulk.

'Yes, let's think of something else, then,' pleaded Smidge. But Karlsson had definitely decided to sulk.

'Watch out I don't fly off and leave you,' he said.

Smidge, Kris, and Jemima all knew what a shame that would be, and they begged Karlsson to stay.

Karlsson sat there for a bit, still looking rather sulky. 'I can't be sure,' he said, 'but I *might* stay if she says "Please, Karlsson," ' he said, pointing at Jemima with his fat little finger.

'Please, Karlsson, do stay so we can have some fun,' she said.

'All right then, I suppose I could,' said Karlsson, and the children breathed a sigh of relief. But they were a bit too hasty.

Smidge's mum and dad often went out for an evening walk. Now Mum was calling from the hall: 'See you in a while! Kris and Jemima can stay until eight, and then you must get straight to bed, Smidge. I'll come in and say goodnight later.'

And they heard the front door slam shut.

'She didn't say how long *I* could stay,' said Karlsson, sticking out his bottom lip. 'Count me out, if things are going to be that unfair.'

'You can stay as long as you like,' said Smidge.

Karlsson stuck his lip out even further.

'Why can't I be driven out at eight like other people?' said Karlsson. 'Count me ou—'

'I'll ask Mum to drive you out at eight,' said Smidge quickly. 'Now what fun shall we come up with?'

Karlsson's bad mood suddenly evaporated.

'We can play ghosts and scare the lives out of people,' he said. 'You lot have no idea what I can do with one little sheet. If I had five öre for every person I've scared the life out of, I'd be able to afford to buy myself tons of toffees. I'm the world's best ghost,' said Karlsson, his eyes sparkling with delight.

Smidge, Kris, and Jemima were keen to play ghosts, but Smidge said, 'We don't need to scare people too much, do we?'

'Easy now, take it easy,' said Karlsson. 'You don't need to teach the world's best ghost anything about haunting. I'm only going to scare the life out of them a *little* bit; they'll hardly notice a thing.'

Karlsson went over to Smidge's bed and pulled off the top sheet.

'This will make a good ghost outfit,' he said.

In Smidge's desk drawer he found a black crayon, which he used to draw a gruesome ghost face on the sheet. Then he got Smidge's scissors and cut two eyeholes, before Smidge could stop him.

'This sheet . . . it's a mere trifle,' said Karlsson. 'And a ghost has got to be able to see, otherwise it might go flapping off and end up in Indo-China or absolutely anywhere.'

Then he threw the sheet over his head like a big hood, with only his podgy little hands sticking out at the sides. Though the children knew it was Karlsson under the sheet, they were still a bit scared, and Woof started barking frantically. It didn't help when the ghost started his motor and went flying off round the ceiling light, the sheet billowing this way and that as he picked up speed. He did look very spooky.

'I'm a little motorized ghost, wild but wonderful,' said Karlsson.

The children stood rooted to the spot, staring at him in alarm. Woof was still barking.

'Really I like to arrive with a bit of a bang,' said Karlsson. 'But if I'm haunting, maybe it's better to switch on the silencer. There!'

And he hovered towards them in virtual silence, and seemed even more ghostly than before.

Now he just had to find someone to haunt.

'I can go and haunt the stairs; someone's bound to come along and get the shock of their life,' said Karlsson.

Then the telephone rang, but Smidge didn't feel like answering it. He let it ring.

Karlsson started trying out some good moans and groans. A ghost that couldn't moan and groan was no use at all, claimed Karlsson, and it was the first thing a little ghost had to learn at ghost school.

All this took time. By the time they were finally standing in the hall, ready to go out to the stairs and start haunting, they heard an odd scratching at the front door. First Smidge thought it was Mum and Dad, back from their walk. But then he saw a long piece of wire being poked through the letterbox. And that made Smidge remember something his dad had read out to Mum from the paper just the other day. The article said how many burglars were about at the moment. The burglars were very clever: they telephoned first, to check whether there was anyone in. If nobody answered, they went straight round to the flat they had rung; then all they had to do was pick the lock on the door and go in and take all the valuables.

Smidge felt terribly frightened when he realized burglars were trying to break in, and so did Kris and Jemima. Kris had shut Woof in Smidge's room so he wouldn't bark while they were haunting, but he was regretting it now.

But Karlsson wasn't the least frightened.

'Easy now, take it easy,' he whispered. 'At times like this, a ghost is the best thing you can have. Come on, let's creep into the sitting room, because I expect that's where your dad keeps his gold ingots and diamonds,' he said to Smidge.

Karlsson and Smidge, Jemima and Kris tiptoed into the sitting room as carefully and quickly and quietly as they could. They crept behind bits of furniture and hid. Karlsson climbed into the lovely old cupboard Mum stored the linen in, and closed the door as best he could. He had scarcely had time to hide before the burglars came sneaking in. Smidge, who was lying behind the sofa by the fireplace, peeped out cautiously. In the middle of the floor stood two burglars, looking thuggish. And— can you imagine it?—it was Rollo and Spike.

'Right, now to find the crown jewels,' said Spike in a low, hoarse voice.

'In there, of course,' said Rollo, pointing to the antique writing desk with all the little drawers. Smidge knew that Mum kept the housekeeping money in one of the drawers, and in another she had the posh, expensive ring and brooch that Granny had given her. And Dad kept the gold medal he had won in a shooting competition there, too. It would be really awful if the burglars took them all, Smidge thought, and he could barely stop himself crying as he lay there behind the sofa.

'You deal with this,' said Spike, 'while I pop out into the kitchen and see if they've got any silver spoons.'

Spike disappeared, and Rollo started pulling out drawers. He whistled with pleasure. He'd found the housekeeping money for sure, thought Smidge, feeling more and more unhappy.

Rollo pulled out the next drawer and whistled again. He must have found the ring and the brooch now.

But then Rollo stopped whistling. Because the door of the linen cupboard opened and a ghost came zooming out with a little groan of warning. And when Rollo turned round and saw the ghost he gave a wheezy gasp, and dropped the money, ring, brooch, and everything else. The ghost fluttered round him, moaning and groaning, and suddenly whizzed off into the kitchen. A second later Spike came sprinting out, white-faced and screaming, 'Gollo, it's a roast!'

He meant 'Rollo, it's a ghost!' but he was so scared it came out as 'Gollo, it's a roast!' instead. It was hardly surprising he was scared, because the ghost was right behind him, moaning and groaning horribly. Rollo and Spike made for the door with the ghost still fluttering about their ears, fled into the hall and straight out of the front door. But the ghost just followed, chasing them down the stairs and shrieking after them in a ghastly, hollow ghost voice:

'Easy now, take it easy! I shall soon catch you up, and then the fun can begin!'

But the ghost got tired of it and came back to the sitting room. Smidge had picked up the housekeeping money, the ring, and the brooch and put them back in the writing desk, and Jemima and Kris had collected up the silver spoons Spike had dropped when he came running in from the kitchen.

'The world's best ghost, that's Karlsson on the Roof,' said the ghost, and took off his ghost outfit.

And the children laughed and felt very relieved, and Karlsson said, 'Nothing beats a ghost, when it comes to scaring burglars. If people knew how well it worked, there'd be an angry little ghost tethered to every safe in town.'

Smidge skipped with delight that Mum's money and brooch and ring and Dad's medal had been saved, and said, 'Imagine people being stupid enough to believe in ghosts! There's no such thing as the supernatural, Dad says.'

He nodded as if to stress what he was saying.

'Stupid burglars, they really thought it was a ghost coming out of the cupboard, when it wasn't anything supernatural at all, just Karlsson on the Roof.'

Karlsson does Magic with a Jiggeryhound

Next morning, a sleepy, tousle-headed little figure in blue and white striped pyjamas came padding barefoot out to the kitchen, where Mum was. Seb and Sally had gone off to school and Dad had left for the office. But Smidge didn't need to go until a bit later, and that was a good thing, because he liked being on his own with Mum for a while in the mornings. Although he was a big boy and had been at school for a while, he still liked sitting on Mum's lap when no one was looking. It was so easy to chat like that, and if they weren't in a hurry, Mum and Smidge would sing together and tell each other stories.

Mum was sitting at the kitchen table reading the newspaper and drinking her coffee. Smidge silently climbed onto her lap and snuggled into her arms, and she held him quietly until he had woken up properly.

Mum and Dad's walk the evening before had taken a bit longer than they intended, and when they got back, Smidge was already in bed, fast asleep. He had kicked off his bedclothes, and when Mum was tucking him back in she noticed that there were two big holes in the sheet, and it was dirty, too. Someone had drawn on it with black crayon. No wonder Smidge had gone off to sleep in such a hurry, thought Mum. But now she had the culprit on her lap, and she wasn't planning to let him go until she had an explanation.

'Now listen, Smidge,' she said, 'I'd really like to know who made those holes in your sheet. And don't try telling me it was Karlsson on the Roof!'

Smidge said nothing, but he was thinking

hard. It *was* Karlsson on the Roof who had made the holes, but he wasn't allowed to say so! In that case it was best to keep quiet about the whole burglar thing as well, because Mum wouldn't believe that either.

'Well,' said Mum when she didn't get an answer.

'Can't you ask Jemima instead?' said Smidge cleverly. Jemima could tell his mum everything that had happened, and she would have to believe *her*.

Oh, so it was Jemima who cut holes in the sheet, thought Mum. And she was proud of Smidge for not telling tales but giving Jemima a chance to own up for herself. Mum gave Smidge a little hug. She decided not to ask any more about the sheet for now, but to have a word with Jemima as soon as she could find her.

'You certainly do like Jemima a lot, don't you?' said Mum.

'Yes, pretty much . . . ' said Smidge.

Mum's eyes were straying to her newspaper again, so Smidge sat quietly on her lap, thinking. Who were the people he really liked? Mum most of all . . . And Dad. He liked Seb and Sally sometimes, well, most of the time in fact . . . especially Seb . . . But sometimes he felt so angry with them he thought he might burst! He liked Karlsson on the Roof. And he liked Jemima . . . pretty much. Maybe he would marry her when he was grown up, because he supposed you had to have a wife, whether you wanted one or not. Though really he'd like to marry Mum better, of course . . . But maybe you weren't allowed to.

When he had got that far, he suddenly had a worrying thought.

'Hey, Mum, if Seb dies when he's grown-up, will I have to marry his wife?'

Mum put down her coffee cup in surprise.

'Whatever makes you think that?' she asked.

She sounded as though she was going to laugh, which made Smidge afraid he'd said something silly, so he didn't want to talk about it any more. But Mum kept on:

'What makes you think that?'

'Well, I've got Seb's old bike,' said Smidge reluctantly. 'And his old skis . . . And those ice skates he had when he was my age . . . and his old pyjamas and gym shoes and everything.'

'But you won't have to have his old wife, I promise you that,' said Mum. And she didn't laugh, luckily.

'Can't I marry you instead?' Smidge suggested.

'I don't know how that would work,' said Mum. 'I'm already married to Dad, you know.'

She was right, of course.

'What bad luck, me and Dad loving the same person,' said Smidge crossly.

But then Mum did laugh, and she said, 'You know what, I rather like it.'

'That's easy for you to say,' said Smidge. 'I'll just have to have Jemima then,' he added. 'Because I suppose everybody has to have someone.'

He thought a bit more, and decided he wouldn't fancy living with Jemima at all. She could be an awkward customer sometimes. And anyway, he wanted to live with Mum and Dad and Seb and Sally. A wife wasn't something he felt he particularly needed.

'I'd much rather have a dog than a wife,' he said. 'Mum, can't I have a dog?'

Mum sighed. Off he went about that blessed dog again! It was almost as wearing as the whole Karlsson on the Roof saga.

'You know what, Smidge, I think it's time you went and got dressed,' said Mum, 'or you'll be late for school.'

'Typical,' said Smidge indignantly. 'When I talk about my dog, you start talking about school.'

But actually it was quite exciting going to school today, because he had such a lot to talk about with Kris and Jemima. They walked home together as usual, and Smidge enjoyed it more than he had for a long time, now that Jemima and Kris knew Karlsson on the Roof as well.

'He's just great all round,' said Jemima. 'Do you think he'll be coming again today?'

'I don't know,' said Smidge. 'He'll only ever say when he's coming *roughly*, and that can mean any time.'

'I hope he comes roughly today,' said Kris. 'Can we come home with you?'

'Of course you can,' said Smidge.

There seemed to be another member of the party, too. Just as the children were about to cross the road, a black poodle puppy came up to Smidge. He nosed the back of Smidge's knee and yapped as if he wanted to be friendly.

'Look, what a dear little dog,' said Smidge, delighted. 'Oh, he must be scared of the traffic, so he wants me to help him cross the road!'

Smidge would gladly have guided him across any number of roads. Maybe the puppy sensed this, because he went trotting over the crossing pressed tightly against Smidge's legs.

'How sweet,' said Jemima. 'Come here, little doggy!'

'No, he wants to be with me,' said Smidge, taking firm hold of the puppy. 'He likes me.'

'He likes me, too, so there,' said Jemima.

The puppy looked as if he liked everyone in the whole world, as long as they liked him. And Smidge liked him, my word how he liked him! He bent down and stroked the puppy and called it and made lots of affectionate little noises, which all meant that this puppy was simply the nicest dog there ever was. The puppy wagged his tail and looked as if he thought so, too. He came yapping and bounding along with the children as they turned into their own road.

A mad hope came over Smidge.

'Maybe he hasn't got anywhere to live,' he

said. 'Maybe he hasn't got anybody to look after him!'

'I bet he has,' said Kris.

'Shut up,' said Smidge angrily. 'How would you know?'

Kris had Woof, so how could he understand what it felt like having no dog of your own, no dog at all!

'Come on, boy,' called Smidge, feeling more and more certain the puppy had nowhere to live.

'Watch out he doesn't follow you home,' said Kris.

'Oh, but I don't mind,' said Smidge. 'I want him to.'

And the puppy came with them. He stayed with them all the way to the entrance of Smidge's flats. Then Smidge gathered him up in his arms and carried him up the stairs.

'I'll ask Mum if I can keep him,' said Smidge eagerly. But Mum wasn't in. There was a note on the kitchen table to say she was down in the laundry room in the basement and Smidge could come down to see her if he needed anything.

But the puppy shot like a rocket straight into Smidge's room, and Smidge, Kris, and Jemima ran after him. Smidge was wild with delight.

'See, he wants to live with me,' he said.

At that very moment, Karlsson on the Roof came puttering in through the window.

'Heysan hopsan,' he shouted. 'Been giving the dog a bath? He seems to have shrunk.'

'Can't you see it's not Woof?' said Smidge. 'This is my dog.'

'Oh no it isn't,' said Kris.

'You haven't got a dog,' said Jemima.

'Me, I've got a thousand dogs up at my house,' said Karlsson. 'The world's best dog handler . . .'

'I didn't see any dogs when I was up there,' said Smidge.

'They were out flying,' Karlsson assured him. 'Mine are flying dogs.'

Smidge wasn't listening to Karlsson. A thousand flying dogs were nothing compared to this cute little puppy.

'I don't think he's got anyone to look after him,' he said again.

Jemima bent down to the dog.

'Well, it says Ahlberg on his collar,' she said.

'I told you,' said Kris. 'They must be the

people who look after him, mustn't they.'

'Ahlberg might have died,' said Smidge.

Whoever Ahlberg was, he didn't like him. But then he had an idea that cheered him up:

'Maybe it's the *dog* that's called Ahlberg,' he said, with a pleading look at Kris and Jemima. They laughed in their annoying way.

'I've got several dogs called Ahlberg,' said Karlsson. 'Heysan hopsan, Ahlberg!'

The puppy jumped up at Karlsson and barked merrily.

'See,' shouted Smidge, 'he knows his name's Ahlberg. Come here, little Ahlberg!'

Jemima gathered up the dog.

'There's a telephone number on his collar, too,' she said heartlessly.

'The dog's got his own telephone,' said Karlsson. 'Tell him to ring home to his housekeeper and tell her he's run off. That's what my dogs do whenever they run off.'

He patted the dog with his plump little hand.

'One of my dogs called Ahlberg ran away just the other day,' said Karlsson. 'So he rang home to tell me. But he had a bit of trouble with the numbers, and he got through to an old major's wife in another part of town, and when she heard it was a dog on the line, she said, "This is the wrong number." And Ahlberg said, "Why did you answer, then?" because he's a clever dog.'

Smidge wasn't listening to Karlsson. Just now the only thing that interested him was the puppy, and he took no notice even when Karlsson said he was in the mood for a bit of fun. But that made Karlsson stick his bottom lip out and say, 'You can count me out, if the dog's all you care about. I need a bit of fun too, you know!'

Kris and Jemima agreed with him.

'We could have a magic show,' said Karlsson, when he had recovered from his sulk. 'The world's best magic maker, guess who that is?'

Smidge, Jemima, and Kris guessed straight away that it must be Karlsson.

'So we'll say a magic show, then,' said Karlsson.

'Yes,' said the children.

'And we'll say it costs a toffee each to get in,' said Karlsson.

'Yes,' said the children.

'And we'll say the toffees all go to a good cause,' said Karlsson.

'Er, well . . . ' said the children doubtfully.

'And there's only one *really* good cause, and that's Karlsson on the Roof,' said Karlsson.

The children looked at each other.

'I don't know . . . ' began Kris.

'We'll *say* that,' shrieked Karlsson, 'or you can count me out!'

So they said the toffees would all go to Karlsson on the Roof.

Kris and Jemima went out into the street to tell all the other children there was going to be a big magic show up at Smidge's. And everyone who still had five öre left of their pocket money ran to the sweet shop and bought their entrance toffees.

The toffees had to be handed over at the door to Smidge's room, where Jemima stood to take them and put them in a box labelled 'For good causes!'

Kris had arranged all the chairs in a row in the middle of the room for the audience to sit on. There was a blanket hung across one corner of the room, and from behind it came whispering and the sound of a dog yapping.

'What are we going to see?' asked a boy called Kevin. 'A load of old rubbish, I bet, and if it is you can give me my toffee back.'

Smidge, Kris, and Jemima didn't like Kevin, because he was always so cocky.

Smidge had stayed behind the blanket, but now he stepped forward. He was holding the puppy in his arms.

'Introducing the world's best magic maker and Ahlberg the jiggeryhound,' he said.

'Like he told you . . . the world's best magic maker,' said a voice from behind the blanket, and out stepped Karlsson. He had Dad's top hat on his head, and draped round his shoulders was Mum's checked apron, tied under his chin in a neat little bow. The apron was meant to look like one of those black capes magicians have.

Everyone clapped except Kevin. Karlsson bowed and looked very pleased with himself. He took off his top hat and showed them it was empty, just like magicians do.

'See for yourselves, ladies and gentlemen,' he said, 'there's nothing in here, nothing at all!'

He's going to pull a rabbit out of the hat,

thought Smidge, because he had once seen a magician do that. It would be fun to see Karlsson produce a rabbit, he thought.

'As I say . . . there's nothing in here,' said Karlsson gloomily. 'And there won't *be* anything in here either, unless you lot put something in,' he went on. 'I see before me lots of greedy little children scoffing toffees. We'll pass the hat round, and you can all put in a toffee. They'll go to a very good cause.'

Smidge went round with the hat, and soon there was a nice little heap of toffees in it. He gave the hat to Karlsson.

'It's got a worrying rattle,' said Karlsson, shaking the hat. 'If it had been full of toffees, it wouldn't have rattled at all.'

He popped one of the toffees into his mouth and started to chew.

'It certainly *feels* as if it's causing me some good,' he said, munching contentedly.

Kevin hadn't put a toffee in the hat, although he had a whole bagful.

'Yes, my friends . . . and Kevin,' said Karlsson. 'Here you see Ahlberg the jiggeryhound. The dog that can do anything. Make a phone call, fly, bake buns, talk, cock his leg . . . anything!'

Just then the poodle puppy really did cock its leg against Kevin's chair, and a small puddle appeared on the floor.

'As you see, I'm not exaggerating,' said Karlsson. 'This dog truly can do anything.'

'Huh,' said Kevin, moving his chair out of the puddle, 'any old dog can do that. But getting it

to talk, that'll be harder, ha ha!'

Karlsson turned to the puppy.

'Do you find talking hard, Ahlberg?'

'Certainly not,' said Ahlberg. 'Well, only when I'm smoking a cigar.'

Smidge, Jemima, and Kris almost jumped out of their skins, because it sounded just as if the dog was talking. But Smidge was pretty sure it was just some trick of Karlsson's. And that was just as well, because Smidge wanted an ordinary dog, not a talking one.

'Now, Ahlberg,' said Karlsson, 'could you please say a bit about the life of a dog for our friends . . . and Kevin?'

'Happy to,' said Ahlberg. And he started telling a story.

'I was at the cinema the other evening,' he said, leaping playfully round Karlsson.

'Ah, you were at the cinema, were you?' said Karlsson.

'Yes, and there were two dog fleas sitting beside me, in the same row,' said Ahlberg.

'Were there indeed?' said Karlsson.

'Yes, and when we came out into the street afterwards, I heard one flea say to the other:

"Shall we *walk* home or take the dog?"'

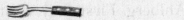

All the children thought it was a good show, even though there wasn't much actual magic in it. Only Kevin sat there with his cocky look.

'Tell him to bake the odd bun while he's at it,' he said with a sneer.

'Do you want to bake the odd bun, Ahlberg?' asked Karlsson.

Ahlberg yawned and lay down on the floor.

'Ha ha, thought so!' said Kevin.

'No, because I forgot to buy any yeast,' said Ahlberg.

All the children liked Ahlberg a lot. But Kevin went on being a nuisance.

'Get him to fly instead, then,' he said. 'You don't need any yeast for that.'

'Do you want to fly, Ahlberg?'

It looked as if Ahlberg might be asleep, but even so he answered when Karlsson spoke to him.

'Yes, I'd be happy to fly,' he said. 'But in that case you'll have to come too, because I promised my mother never to go up on my own.'

'Come on then, little Ahlberg,' said Karlsson, gathering up the puppy in his arms.

And a second later they were flying, Karlsson and Ahlberg. First they went up to the ceiling and did a few circuits of the light, and then they flew off out of the window. That made even Kevin go pale with astonishment.

All the children rushed to the window and stood there watching Karlsson and Ahlberg hover off over the rooftops. But Smidge shouted desperately:

'Karlsson, Karlsson, come back here with my dog!'

And Karlsson did. He was soon back, and he put Ahlberg down on the floor. Ahlberg shook himself and looked so surprised, you might almost have thought it was the first flight of his life.

'I'm afraid that's it for today. We've no more to show you,' said Karlsson. 'But *you* have,' he said, giving Kevin a little nudge.

Kevin didn't understand what he meant.

'Toffee,' said Karlsson.

So Kevin got out his paper bag and gave the whole thing to Karlsson, though he did help himself to a toffee first.

'Never seen such a greedy boy,' said Karlsson. Then he looked round eagerly. 'Where's the box for good causes?' he asked.

Jemima went to fetch it. Karlsson was bound to offer the toffees round, she thought, now he had so many. But Karlsson didn't. He took the box and counted all his toffees hungrily.

'Fifteen,' he said. 'Enough for my supper! Heysan hopsan, I've got to get home for my supper!'

With that, Karlsson vanished out of the window.

All the children had to go home, including Jemima and Kris.

Smidge and Ahlberg were left alone, and Smidge really liked that. He held the puppy in his arms and whispered things to him. And the puppy licked his face, and then went to sleep. He made little snuffling noises as he slept.

But then Mum came up from the laundry room, and everything went terribly wrong. Mum didn't agree at all that Ahlberg had nowhere else to live. She rang the telephone number on the dog collar, and said her little boy had found a black poodle puppy.

Smidge stood by the phone with Ahlberg in his arms, whispering frantically:

'Please, God, let it not be their puppy!'

But it *was* their puppy.

'Darling,' said Mum after she hung up. 'It's a boy called Simon Ahlberg who owns Bobby.'

'Bobby?' asked Smidge.

'Yes, that's the puppy's name. Simon's been crying all afternoon. He's coming for Bobby at seven o'clock.'

Smidge said nothing, but he went whiter in the face, and his eyes glistened. He hugged the puppy, and when Mum wasn't listening he whispered in its ear:

'Dear little Ahlberg, I want you to be my dog.'

But at seven o'clock Simon Ahlberg came for his puppy. Then Smidge shut himself in his room and lay sobbing his heart out.

Karlsson goes to a Birthday Party

Summer had arrived, school was over, and Smidge would soon be off to Granny's. But first something very important had to happen. Smidge was going to be eight. Oh, he'd been waiting so long for this birthday . . . almost since his last one! It was curious how long it was between birthdays, almost as long as between Christmases.

The evening before his birthday, he had a little chat with Karlsson.

'I'm having a birthday party,' said Smidge. 'Jemima and Kris are coming round, and we're going to have the party food here, in my room . . .'

Smidge hesitated and looked glum.

'I so much want to invite you, as well,' he said, 'but . . . '

Mum was so angry with Karlsson on the Roof, that was the problem. There was no point asking her if Karlsson could come to the birthday party.

But Karlsson stuck his bottom lip out even further than ever.

'Count me out, if you can't count me in,' he said. '*I* need a bit of fun, too, you know!'

'All right, you can come,' said Smidge quickly. He'd talk to Mum—whatever she said. He just couldn't have a birthday party without Karlsson.

'What will we be having to eat?' asked Karlsson, once he'd got over his sulk.

'Cake, of course,' said Smidge. 'I'm having a birthday cake with eight candles on.'

'Ah,' said Karlsson. 'Can I suggest something?'

'What?' asked Smidge.

'Can't you ask your mum to let you have *eight* cakes and *one* candle instead?'

Smidge didn't think Mum would let him.

'Will you be getting any nice presents, then?'

'I don't know,' said Smidge.

He sighed. He knew very well what he wanted— more than anything else in the world. But he wouldn't get it.

'I'm sure I won't be getting a dog as long as I live,' he said. 'But I'll get lots of other presents. So I've decided I'm going be in a good mood anyway and not think about the dog all day.'

'No, and you've always got me,' said Karlsson. 'I should think that counts for a lot more than a dog!'

He put his head on one side and looked at Smidge.

'I wonder what presents you'll get,' he said. 'I wonder if you'll get any toffee. If you do, I think it should go straight to good causes.'

'Don't worry, if I get a bag of toffees I'll give it to you,' said Smidge.

He would have done anything for Karlsson, especially now they were about to be parted.

'Karlsson, the day after tomorrow I'm going away to Granny's for the whole summer,' said Smidge.

This made Karlsson look a bit gloomy to start with, but then he said importantly, *'I'm* going to *my* granny's, too. She's much grannier than yours.' 'Where does she live, your granny?' asked Smidge.

'In a house,' said Karlsson. 'Did you think she spent her nights running about without a roof over her head?'

There wasn't time to say much more about Karlsson's granny or Smidge's birthday presents or anything, because it was getting late and Smidge had to get to bed, so he would wake up in good time on his birthday.

Those minutes, when you were lying there waiting for the door to open and everybody to come in—with a birthday breakfast tray and presents and everything—were almost too much to bear. Smidge's tummy was tying itself in knots with excitement.

But now they were coming, starting to sing 'Happy birthday' outside the door, and the door was opening. And there they all were, Mum and Dad and Seb and Sally.

Smidge sat bolt upright in bed, his eyes sparkling. 'Many happy returns, Smidge darling,' said Mum.

They all wished him a happy birthday. And there was the cake with the eight candles, and presents on the tray.

Quite a few presents. But not really as many as he *usually* got on his birthday. There were no more than four parcels, however Smidge counted them. But Dad said, 'There might be a few more presents turning up later on. You don't need all your presents first thing in the morning, do you?'

And Smidge was pleased with his four parcels. He had a paint box and a toy pistol and a book and a new pair of jeans, and he liked them all. They were very kind, Mum and Dad and Seb and Sally! Nobody had such kind parents and brothers and sisters as him.

He fired a few pretend shots with his pistol, and it made a good bang. His whole family sat on the edge of his bed listening, and oh how much he liked them all!

'Just think that eight whole years have passed since this little chap came into the world,' said Dad.

'Yes,' said Mum. 'How time flies! Do you remember how hard it was raining here in

Stockholm that day?'

'Mum, I was born in Stockholm, wasn't I?' asked Smidge.

'You certainly were,' said Mum.

'But Seb and Sally, they were born in Malmö?'

'Yes they were.'

'And you, Dad, you were born in Gothenburg, you said.'

'Yes, I'm a Gothenburg boy,' said Dad.

'And where were you born, Mum?'

'In Eskilstuna,' said Mum.

Smidge threw his arms round her neck.

'Well, what astronomically good luck that we all met up!'

Everybody agreed. And they sang 'Happy birthday' to Smidge again, and he fired his pistol with a huge bang.

He had plenty of chances to play with his pistol as the day went by and he waited for it to be time for his party. And he had plenty of time to think about what Dad had said . . . that there could be more presents turning up later on. For one short, blissful moment he wondered whether a miracle might happen and he might get a dog after all, but he knew all along that it was impossible. And he told himself off for imagining anything so silly—he'd decided, hadn't he, that he wouldn't think about dogs on his birthday, but stay in a good mood?

And Smidge *was* in a good mood. As the afternoon wore on, Mum started setting the special table in his room. She put lots of flowers on the table and the best pink cups—three of them.

'Mum, we need four cups,' said Smidge.

'Oh, why?' asked Mum in surprise.

Smidge swallowed hard. He would have to tell her he'd invited Karlsson on the Roof, even though Mum would be bound not to like it.

'Karlsson on the Roof's coming too,' said Smidge, looking Mum in the eye.

'Ahhh,' said Mum, 'I see! But all right, since it's your birthday.'

She patted Smidge on his little blond head.

'What a lot of babyish ideas you come up with, Smidge. Nobody would think you were turning eight today . . . how old are you really?'

'I'm a man in my prime,' said Smidge solemnly. 'And so is Karlsson.'

Smidge's birthday was going at a snail's pace.

It was 'later on' all right, but he still hadn't spotted any more presents.

In the end he got one, at any rate. Seb and Sally hadn't broken up for the summer holidays yet, and when they got home from school they shut themselves in Seb's room. Smidge wasn't allowed in. He could hear them giggling in there, and rustling paper. Smidge was dying to know what they were doing.

After quite some time they came out, and Sally laughed and handed him a parcel. Smidge was delighted, and was about to tear off the paper, but Seb said, 'You have to read the poem on it first.'

They had written in big, clear letters so Smidge would be able to read it for himself, and he read:

'All the time you nag and fuss,
That you want a dog from us.
Now Sis and Bro are being kind,
Since we can't get it off our mind,
So we have bought a lovely pet.
Just how generous can we get?
This cuddly little puppy toy

148

Is bound to make you shout for joy.
He doesn't bark or jump at all,
Or leave big puddles in the hall.'

Smidge just stood there, without a word.

'Open your present, then,' said Seb. But Smidge threw it on the floor and burst into tears.

'Oh, Smidge, what's the matter?' cried Sally.

'Have we upset you?' said Seb unhappily.

Sally threw her arms round Smidge.

'We're so sorry. We were only teasing, you know.'

Smidge wrenched himself free. The tears were streaming down his cheeks.

'But you *knew*,' he sobbed, 'you *knew* I wanted a real dog, so why did you tease me?'

He rushed into his room and threw himself on the bed. Seb and Sally came after him, and Mum came running, too. But Smidge took no notice. He was sobbing and shaking. Now his whole birthday was ruined. He'd decided to stay in a good mood although he wasn't getting a puppy, but when they came along with a *cuddly toy* dog . . . His tears turned to wails as he thought about it, and he burrowed his face as far into his pillow as he could. Mum and Seb and Sally stood round the bed, looking upset.

'I'd better ring Dad and ask him to come home from the office a bit early,' said Mum.

Smidge carried on crying . . . how would Dad coming home early help?

Everything was awful now, and his birthday was ruined. Nothing would help.

He heard Mum going to make the call . . . But he carried on crying. A bit later, he heard Dad arrive home. But he carried on crying. He would never be happy again. It would be better if he died, then Seb and Sally could have his cuddly toy dog and never, ever forget how cruel they'd been to their little brother on his birthday, while he was alive.

Then suddenly they were all gathered round his bed—Mum and Dad and Seb and Sally. He buried his face even deeper in his pillow.

'Smidge, there's someone waiting for you out in the hall,' said Dad.

Smidge didn't answer. Dad shook him by the shoulder.

'Didn't you hear? There's a little friend of

yours out in the hall.'

'Is it Kris or Jemima?' muttered Smidge peevishly.

'No, it's someone called Bumble,' murmured Mum.

'I don't know anyone called Bumble,' muttered Smidge even more crossly.

'Maybe not,' said Mum, 'but he very much wants to get to know *you*.'

Just then there was a short, yapping bark from the hall.

Smidge tensed all his muscles and gripped the pillow hard . . . no, he simply mustn't start imagining things!

But the yapping bark came again. Smidge sat up in bed with a jerk.

'Is it a dog?' he asked. 'Is it a real, live dog?'

'Yes, it's *your* dog,' said Dad.

Then Seb dashed out into the hall, and a second later he was back, and in his arms was— oh, it couldn't be true!—a little, wirehaired dachshund puppy.

'Is this a real live dog for *me*?' whispered Smidge.

He still had tears in his eyes as he held out

his arms for Bumble. He looked as if he thought the puppy might vanish in a puff of smoke any moment.

But Bumble didn't vanish. Bumble was in his arms, and Bumble licked his face and whimpered and barked and snapped at his ears.

Bumble was a totally, stupendously live dog.

'Happy now, Smidge?' asked Dad.

Smidge sighed. How could Dad think he needed to ask? He was so happy that it hurt deep inside his soul or his tummy or wherever it is that hurts when you're really happy.

'You know that stuffed toy dog was meant for Bumble to play with, don't you?' said Sally. 'We didn't mean to tease you . . . much,' she added.

Smidge forgave them everything. And anyway, he was scarcely listening to Sally. He was busy talking to Bumble.

'Bumble, Bumble, you're my dog.'

Then he said to Mum:

'I think Bumble's even nicer than Ahlberg. Because wirehaired dachshunds are definitely the best.'

Then he remembered that Kris and Jemima

would be coming any minute. Oh, he could hardly believe you could have so much fun on a single day. And just imagine, they would see that he now had a dog which really *was* all his own, and the dearest, nicest, sweetest one on earth.

But then he had a worrying thought.

'Mum, will I be able to take Bumble when we go to Granny's?'

'Yes of course. You can have him in this little basket on the train,' said Mum, pointing to a dog basket that Seb had just fetched from the hall.

'Ohhh,' sighed Smidge, 'ohhh!'

Just then there was a ring at the door. It was Jemima and Kris, and Smidge went rushing up to them, shouting, 'I've got a dog! My very own dog!'

'Ooh, he's so sweet,' said Jemima. But then she remembered why she was there and said, 'Happy birthday! This is from me and Kris.'

She gave Smidge a bag of toffees. Then she launched herself at Bumble, and shrieked again:

'Ooh, he's so sweet.'

That was what Smidge liked to hear.

'Nearly as nice as Woof,' said Kris.

'Nicer, really,' said Jemima. 'Nicer than

Ahlberg, even.'

'Yes, much nicer than Ahlberg,' said Kris.

Smidge thought Jemima and Kris were both being really kind. He invited them to sit down at the tea table.

Mum had just put out delicious little ham and cheese sandwiches and lots of cakes and biscuits. And in the middle of the table stood the birthday cake with the eight candles.

Mum was just coming in from the kitchen with a big jug full of hot chocolate. She started filling their cups straight away.

'Aren't we going to wait for Karlsson?' asked Smidge cautiously.

Mum shook her head.

'Let's not bother about Karlsson. You know what, I'm pretty sure he won't be coming. We just won't bother about him from now on. Because you've got Bumble now, after all.'

Yes, he had Bumble now, after all . . . But that was no reason why he wouldn't want Karlsson at his party.

Jemima and Kris sat down at the table, and Mum offered round the sandwiches. Smidge put Bumble in his little basket and came to join them. Mum went out of the room, leaving the children on their own.

Seb stuck his nose round the door and said, 'Make sure you save some cake for Sally and me!'

'I suppose I'd better,' said Smidge. 'But it's not fair really, because you had seven or eight years of eating cake before I was even born.'

'Don't push your luck; I want a big slice,' said Seb and shut the door.

He had hardly gone before they heard the familiar whirr, and in came Karlsson.

'You started without me?' he shouted. 'How much have you eaten?'

Smidge soothed him by saying they hadn't eaten anything yet.

'Good,' said Karlsson.

'Aren't you going to wish Smidge a happy birthday?' asked Jemima.

'Oh . . . er . . . yes, happy birthday,' said Karlsson. 'Where shall I sit?'

There was no cup for Karlsson, of course, and when he noticed he stuck out his bottom lip and looked sulky.

'Count me out, if things are going to be so *unfair*. Why didn't *I* get a cup?'

Smidge quickly gave Karlsson his. Then he tiptoed out to the kitchen to get another cup for himself.

'Karlsson, I've got a dog,' he said as he came back in. 'He's over there, and he's called Bumble.'

Smidge pointed to Bumble, who had fallen asleep in his basket.

'Oh, that's nice,' said Karlsson. 'Bags I *that* sandwich . . . and *that* one . . . and *that* one!'

'Oops, I nearly forgot,' he added. 'I've got a birthday present for you, too, I'm the kindest person there is.'

He fished a whistle out of his trouser pocket and gave it to Smidge.

'You can whistle to Bumble with it. I often whistle to my dogs, too, though mine are called Ahlberg and can fly.'

'Are they all called Ahlberg?' asked Kris.

'Yes, all thousand of them. When are we starting on the birthday cake?'

'Thank you so much for the whistle, Karlsson, it's really nice of you,' said Smidge. It was going to be such fun whistling to Bumble with it.

'But I might borrow it sometimes,' said

Karlsson. 'Quite often, in fact,' he said, and went on anxiously, 'Did you get any toffee?'

'Oh yes,' said Smidge, 'I had some from Jemima and Kris.'

'That can go straight to good causes,' said Karlsson, grabbing the bag. He stuffed it in his pocket, and then attacked the sandwiches.

Jemima, Kris, and Smidge could see they would have to be quick if they wanted any. But luckily Mum had made lots.

Mum and Dad and Seb and Sally were in the sitting room.

'Sounds as though they're having fun in there,' said Mum. 'Oh, I'm so glad Smidge has got his dog. It'll mean a lot of work, of course, but it can't be helped.'

'Yes, I'm sure he'll forget all his daft fantasies about Karlsson on the Roof now,' said Dad.

There were voices and laughter coming from Smidge's room, and Mum said, 'Shall we pop in for a look? They're so cute, the children!'

'Yes, let's go and have a look,' said Sally.

So they all went, Mum and Dad and Seb and Sally, to take a peep at Smidge's birthday party.

It was Dad who opened the door. But it was
Mum who screamed first. Because she was the
first one to catch sight of the fat little man
sitting beside Smidge.

A fat little man, up to his ears in cream cake.

'I think I'm going to faint,' said Mum.

Dad and Seb and Sally stood rooted to the
spot, staring.

'Karlsson did come after all, see, Mum,' said Smidge happily. 'Oh, what a birthday this has turned out to be.'

The fat little man wiped some of the cake from around his mouth and then waved to Dad and Mum and Seb and Sally with a podgy hand, spraying cream in all directions.

'Heysan hopsan,' he shouted. 'I don't think you've had the pleasure before, have you? My name is Karlsson on the Roof . . . Now, now, Jemima, don't take too much, I'm supposed to get a bit of cake too, aren't I?'

And he grabbed Jemima's hand, which was holding the cake slice, and made her drop it.

'Never seen such a greedy little girl,' he said

Then he helped himself to a huge piece.

'The world's best cake eater, that's Karlsson on the Roof,' he said, and smiled a sunny smile.

'Let's go,' whispered Mum.

'Yes, don't let me stop you,' said Karlsson.

'Promise me one thing,' Dad said to Mum when they had closed the door behind them, 'all of you, Seb and Sally too! Don't tell *anybody* about this, not *anybody*!'

'Why not?' said Seb.

'Nobody would believe you,' said Dad. 'But if they *did*, we wouldn't get a minute's peace for the rest of our lives.'

Dad and Mum and Seb and Sally shook on it and promised not to tell another soul about the strange playmate Smidge had found himself.

And they kept their word. No one has ever heard them say a single word about Karlsson. That means Karlsson can carry on living up in the little house nobody knows about, although it's on the ordinary roof of an ordinary house in a perfectly ordinary street in Stockholm. Karlsson is free to go around jiggery-poking in peace and quiet, which is exactly what he does do. Because he's the world's best jiggerypoker.

When all the sandwiches were gone, and all the cakes and biscuits and the whole birthday cake, and Jemima and Kris had gone home and Bumble was asleep, Smidge said goodbye to Karlsson. Karlsson was sitting on the window ledge, ready to launch himself off. The curtains were swaying gently and the air was so warm, because it was summer, after all.

'Please, Karlsson, dear Karlsson, you will definitely still be living on the roof when I get back from Granny's, won't you?' said Smidge.

'Easy now, take it easy,' said Karlsson. 'As long as my granny lets me. But I can't be sure she will. Because she thinks I'm the world's best grandson.'

'And are you?' asked Smidge.

'Yes, who on earth else could be? Can *you* think of anyone?' asked Karlsson.

Then he turned the winder that was somewhere just in front of his tummy button. His propellor started to whirr.

'When I come back, we'll eat lots of cake,' he shouted, 'because what we've just had wasn't enough to make *anyone* fat. Heysan hopsan, Smidge!'

'Heysan hopsan, Karlsson,' shouted Smidge And Karlsson was gone.

But in the little dog basket beside Smidge's bed, Bumble lay sleeping. Smidge leant over him. He breathed in the smell of him. He stroked one dry little hand gently over the puppy's head.

'Bumble, we're off to Granny's tomorrow,' he

said. 'Good night, Bumble! Sleep well, boy!'

Ever since Karlsson flew in through Smidge's window, they've been firm friends; even though Karlsson gets Smidge into trouble sometimes! Zoom through their adventures with them as they fly over rooftops, gobble cream buns, play pranks, and frighten the babysitter.

Ever since Karlsson flew in through Smidge's window, they've been firm friends; even though Karlsson gets Smidge into trouble sometimes! Zoom through their adventures with them as they fly over rooftops, gobble cream buns, play pranks, and frighten the babysitter.

The paper is offering a reward to whoever can catch the mysterious flying object spotted over the city rooftops. Will the world finally discover Karlsson, or can Smidge protect his friend?

ABOUT THE AUTHOR

Astrid Lindgren was born in 1907, and grew up at a farm called Näs in the south of Sweden. Her first book was published in 1944, followed a year later by *Pippi Longstocking*. She wrote 34 chapter books and 41 picture books, that all together have sold 165 million copies worldwide. Her books have been translated into 107 different languages and according to UNESCO's annual list, she is the 18th most translated author in the world.

She created stories about Pippi, a free-spirited, red-haired girl to entertain her daughter, Karin, who was ill with pneumonia. The girl's name 'Pippi Longstocking' was in fact invented by Karin. Astrid Lindgren once commented about her work, 'I write to amuse the child within me, and can only hope that other children may have some fun that way, too.'

For more information visit **www.astridlindgren.com**